Puck and Make Up

Rush Hockey #7

Elise Faber

PUCK AND MAKE UP
BY ELISE FABER

Newsletter sign-up

NO PUCKS LOST BETWEEN US
Copyright © 2024 Elise Faber
Print ISBN-13: 978-1-63749-131-7
Ebook ISBN-13:978-1-63749-130-0

Rush Hockey

ONE

FOX

I want to rinse my eyes out with acid.

Then gouge them from their sockets with a spoon.

Because—

I gag.

I *had* been worried about my best friend—and teammate—Joel, who spent the afternoon in a meeting with management of the Rush Hockey team we both play for.

He was thinking this might be it.

That they weren't going to renew his contract.

That this was going to be the end of his career.

Something I was feeling more than a little guilty about.

Because *I'd* just gotten the best news.

I'm getting a contract to the big leagues.

Not the Gold as I'd expected, but the Grizzlies—one of the newest teams in the league. Still local. Still fucking awesome. Still everything I've always wanted. Only...my news was tempered by concern for my friend.

Would he be done?

Would he be *okay* with being done?

So, when I ran into Joel's girlfriend, Billie Rose—or Rosie as we all call her—and saw the look in her eyes when she came into Monroe's, looking for Joel after his meeting...

I couldn't shake the feeling that it had all gone wrong.

So, I texted.

But she didn't reply.

Neither had Joel.

Or picked up any of my calls.

And trouble follows those two like it's a goddamned note taped to each of their backs.

So...I went to their house, intending to take a peek inside, to make sure they connected and were both okay.

And—

I shudder.

Well, I sure as shit had gotten my *peek*.

And more.

Much more.

I gag again, shake myself, and keep making my way along the tree line.

Keep making my way *through* the trees, to the spot I need to check.

Because there's another reason I'm on this side of town, another reason I'm well away from my apartment in downtown River's Bend.

An apartment I just broke my lease on because I'm going to the Grizzlies.

Finally, I'm getting a contract.

Finally, I'm going to consistently play at the highest level of hockey possible.

Just...not tonight.

Tonight I'm dealing with acid-filled eyes and spoons made for gouging and a sick feeling in the pit of my stomach that has nothing to do with walking in on my friends fucking.

With handcuffs.

Another shudder.

"Focus," I mutter, even though I don't want to, even though I've been avoiding thinking about this shit for far too fucking long—not wanting to admit what has been right in front of me...

Even though it's been *right in front of me.*

And then, last week, I confirmed it.

But I couldn't do anything about it—not with all the shit swirling through River's Bend, not with my friends finally having a moment of peace.

Not with...

Dessie being Dessie.

She's beautiful and stubborn and I want nothing more than for her to be mine...

And she hates me.

I curse under my breath, knowing this is all a nightmare that's going to blow up on me, doing more damage than acid and dull spoons.

But still, I don't stop walking.

Don't stop moving to the spot the note had indicated I come to.

It had been slipped under the windshield wiper of my car when I was parked outside Monroe's, so the intelligence of me following that written order by an unknown person was...well, debatable.

"Probably going to get murdered out here," I mutter as I move along the trail. "Or the guys are waiting around the corner, ready to prank me."

Only...I know it's neither of those.

Because when I round the corner of the trail, eyes having long adjusted to the dark, I can easily see the person silhouetted against the moonlight in the small clearing.

A clearing I vaguely remember.

From decades before.

The person on the other side of it turns, and I feel that same gut punch as I experienced the first time I saw her in town when I was traded to the Rush a few seasons back.

Only this blow is more powerful.

I knew for *certain* now.

Before it had been an odd familiarity.

Now it's...

Fact.

And it's why I move close enough to see her face, her expression, her eyes that are a familiar shade of blue I've seen often during my time in River's Bend.

It's why I move close to Annie Donovan.

It's why I move close to *Rosie's* mother, who's also...

"Hi, Mom."

My mother.

She opens her mouth to reply—

A gasp.

Only, it's not from Annie. It comes from *behind me.*

I turn...

To find Dessie standing directly behind me.

Two

DESSIE

"What the fuck?" I ask, digging into my pocket and pulling out my phone. "What the *actual* fuck?"

I jab at the screen and hit my best friend in the world, Rosie's, number.

It starts ringing.

And, thankfully, since she pretty much always picks up my calls, this time is no different, though she *is* out of breath when she answers, "Des?"

"I need you and Joel to get your asses out to Reacher's clearing." A beat. "Like five minutes ago."

There's a brief pause. Then, "Got it."

The call disconnects and I'm staring at the woman who almost fucked over my friend's life—Annie Donovan is no peach, even though she spent a lot of her life trapped in a toxic relationship with Rosie's dad (who's now in prison for trying to frame Rosie to take the fall for his crimes). She's a victim, but also complicit in hurting my friend.

And...Fox is here saying—

I clamp my teeth together.

I shake my head.

That can't be right.

It doesn't make sense.

I shove that aside. I'll deal with him in a minute.

"I thought you skipped town?" I ask Annie after we've all stood around, staring at each other for far too long.

"I-I came back," Rosie's mom says.

"Why?" Joel asks. "Why now?"

And why do I feel like that's a question loaded with so many undertones I can't even begin to tease them apart?

I lift my chin, glare at him.

He's a liar. That's the only thing that matters.

"I needed you," Annie says, her voice about as strong as a dried blade of glass. "But I—" She slides a step back, as though she's going to disappear into the trees.

I open my mouth, reach out a hand—

Fox snags her shoulder instead. "No," he mutters. "You are so not running from this again."

"Y-you're my son. You have to help me."

My heart squeezes hard enough that I actually feel light-headed, and I must make a sound because Fox whips his head in my direction. "I've only known for a few days," he says. "I—" He closes his eyes for a moment. "I always knew I was adopted. I just...didn't know my birth mother was...*her.*"

I inhale, but I don't get the chance to reply because there's a noise from behind me.

We all turn and see Rosie standing at the edge of the clearing, Joel at her side. Their hair is disheveled, and I think that she's wearing shoes that don't match, but they're here...

And in less than ten minutes.

They made good time.

My friend opens her mouth, closes it, at a loss for words for once.

Joel isn't, though, and he tucks Rosie behind him before growling, "What the fuck, Fox?"

Annie's shoulders hunch at the tone, already retreating into herself.

But Fox just turns to face us. "I'll explain. I just...needed to see for myself."

"See what?" Joel growls. He looks ready to kill, and I don't blame him.

Except, I can't deny that my heart squeezes at the look on Fox's face.

"We shouldn't do this here," Fox says quietly.

"I think—" Rosie closes her eyes. "That here is as good as anywhere."

I move to her, take her hand, feel that she's trembling.

"Rosie," Joel begins.

She leans against me, opens her eyes then turns to Fox. "Please...just tell me?"

The expression on Annie Donovan's face says she's going to be stubborn—that breakable reed turning to steel.

It doesn't ever last long.

But, of course, she summons it for this moment.

Thankfully, though, Fox isn't holding back.

"You know I'm adopted," he says.

Joel nods tersely but Rosie's eyes widen slightly in surprise—the same reaction I'd had to him talking about his *birth* mother. All I've known about Fox's family is that he has a good relationship with his parents. I just...didn't realize they weren't his bio ones.

"My parents did one of those tests, the DNA ones. They were curious, and I have to admit I was too. So I bought one and sent it in." He exhales. "And when the results came in, it turned out my biological mother is..." He flicks his gaze down to the woman he's practically holding up now.

Annie jerks.

"What the fuck?" Joel whispers.

Exactly.

"I only just found out, and I know that I needed to tell you guys," he says, "but there's been a lot going on and with the contracts and—"

It's dark, but there's enough moonlight that I swear his cheeks have gone pink.

"—well, I also didn't know *how* to tell you that—" He lifts one big, broad shoulder, drops it.

Rosie exhales. "So...you're my brother?"

"Half."

We all still, glance over at Annie.

That slender thread of steel makes an appearance.

"Half," she repeats. "Your father..." Her eyes drift to Rosie's and the steel immediately begins to melt, the wilting violet that I've associated with Annie Donovan coming back full force. Tears sink heavily into her words, making her voice falter and turn whiny. "I wanted to keep you, but after he died, my parents made me choose. Give you up or they'd disown me."

"After *who* died, Mom?" Rosie presses when Annie doesn't go on.

"Nathan," she says quietly. "I was...we were supposed to get married. Then he was in a car accident, and I was—" She shakes her head. "I had to make a choice."

There's a long pause, and I don't miss the sliver of pain that slices across Fox's face.

Clearly, she'd chosen to give him up.

Chosen her future over her son's.

Hurt more people she's supposed to love.

I want to throttle her.

"But," Fox says quietly into that taut silence, "I've met you once before."

Her eyes close and she's silent for a long, long moment before she says, "John gave me that gift." Her throat works. "He knew your family was camping in the area and...engineered a meeting."

Joel curses quietly.

But I'm watching Fox, watching his eyes close again.

Fuck, he really hadn't known any of this before, had he?

"I remembered," he whispers. "When I first saw you in town, when Rosie introduced us, I had this flash of a memory, of familiarity. I just...it didn't make sense until the test results came in."

My insides twist.

"Exactly how long have you known Fox was your son, Mom?" Rosie asks quietly.

Joel stills. Fox jerks. I have to bite back a gasp.

But Annie...well, I practically see the fog she uses as a defense mechanism sweep up around her. She uses it to hide, to avoid...

Situations exactly like this.

"Mom," Rosie snaps, clearly noticing the same thing. "Keep it together for-fucking-once and just answer the question."

Annie shakes her head.

"*Mom.*"

Annie jumps, but then the words rush out of her. "Your father arranged the trade in exchange for the contract to the rink."

Fox jerks again.

"I love watching you play," she whispers. "You're big and strong. So much like Billie"—her deceased son, a loss we'd always thought was responsible for her mental breakdown in the first place—"would have been." That fog creeps in further, the grief that had broken her so much clearer now.

She'd lost not just one son.

But *two*.

And because of that...

She lost a daughter.

Rosie's shaking and I wrap my arm around her waist.

But she's tough. She keeps it together.

"Secrets," she whispers. "It's always fucking secrets with you. Why couldn't you ever just have a conversation with me? With us?" she adds, glancing at Fox.

And my insides twist again.

Because that's our Rosie—generous and sweet with a huge heart. Fox has already been part of her family, but this...

Well, the news may have thrown her, but she won't hold it against him.

I know that with complete certainty.

And even though Fox pushes every button of mine—for *reasons*—I know I can't hold this against him either.

Not with the pain in his eyes and the worry etched into his face.

"We don't talk about it," Annie whispers. "N-not ever. We move f-forward a-and—" Her voice breaks. "We don't look back."

"Except, the past has a funny way of showing back up," Joel mutters.

But Annie's expression has smoothed out, and I know she doesn't process the jab at all, same as she barely processes Fox saying, "That's all of it—at least from me."

Rosie exhales shakily.

"And it's late, we should finish this conversation somewhere else."

"Right," Joel says. "You take that one. I'll get these two."

THREE

"That's not how you do it," the beautiful goddess next to me says, yanking the spoon from my hands and elbowing me out of the way.

I smother a sigh, but allow the woman, who's tall and strong, but nowhere near as tall and strong as I am, to shove me to the side, knowing that this is just Dessie.

Or maybe, this is just Dessie with *me*.

She's beautiful, full of lean curves and lithe muscles that give hint to her former career—a firefighter battling blazes, at least before she up and quit for some reason that she won't share with anyone. And she's got height, towering over her friends.

But she's still tiny when compared to me.

Because I'm a fucking behemoth.

Six-five.

Six-eight on skates.

So even as she's shoving me out of the way, she's doing it from nearly a foot beneath me.

And I'm letting her.

Because ever since the truth has come out about my birth mother, the hatred that Dessie has for me is...

Tempered.

Oh, she still gives me sass and her wit is full of sharp edges rather than gentle teasing.

But she's different.

Same as Rosie's been different since she found out the truth.

They're all looking at me like I'm fragile.

Like I'm going to snap and freak out and—

Well, pull an Annie Donovan.

At least it won't be much longer before I head down to San Jose, before I get some space.

Of course, it's not going to be far from my Rosie, seeing as how Joel's career isn't over and he's heading down to San Francisco.

At least the handcuff incident I witnessed—the one that led to acid-filled eyes I wanted to gouge out with a spoon—from a couple weeks ago was worth it.

Joel got a contract too.

He's going to the Gold.

From teammates to rivals.

That's a hockey player's reality.

"You know," I mutter, leaning back against the counter and fixing my stare on Dessie, focusing on the here and now because if I stop and think about the rest of it, I want to punch something. "*I'm* the one who was trusted with making the chocolate chip cookies in the first place."

I know it's because they're trying to giving me something to do so I'm not focusing on the fact that Annie Donovan has disappeared again.

And so I'm also not fixated on figuring out how to tell my actual parents—and not my fucking egg donor—about the circumstances of my ending up in River's Bend in the first place.

Or *if* I should tell them at all.

Especially considering that creating a relationship with my birth mom isn't high up on my list of priorities.

She's...well, I feel sorry for her.

But do I seriously want a relationship with a person who treated Rosie like she had?

Who'd made it clear that she looks after herself first and foremost?

I've built a family here.

I have great parents.

I don't need Annie Donovan.

And I—

Cookies!

And I need to focus on the fucking cookies and stop spending so much time in my head.

These cookies are my specialty.

I can't make many things—or at least not all that many that are edible—but my chocolate chip cookies are the shit. Ooey, gooey and with just the perfect hint of salt so that the sweet doesn't overwhelm.

My grandma taught me the recipe.

I just...perfected it.

So, the lean, grumpy goddess trying to take over the one thing I can control right now isn't all that helpful.

We're at Bailey and Axel's ranch house on the edge of River's Bend, the sprawling cattle farm settled against the foothills of the Sierra Nevada Mountains. It's not far from my apartment closer to town (the one I only have for a couple more weeks), but it may as well be on another planet with its wide porch looking out onto acres and acres of grazing land. The rest of the guys—Axel, Joel, and Ryan—are currently hanging out around a small, landscaped patch, enjoying the warm evening air, playing games with Rosie, Bailey, and Veronica.

Along with Dessie.

Except, now she's in the kitchen, taking over.

Training camp starts in a couple weeks and with us now on three different teams, I know we won't have many opportunities to get together like this again any time soon.

I want to make it count.

Only now, I'm stuck in the kitchen with a woman who can't stand me as she tells me I don't know how to make chocolate chip cookies.

I smother a grin.

Okay, fine.

There's never an instance where I don't like being close to Dessie.

Yeah, she pushes my buttons.

Yeah, sometimes I want to throttle her.

But there hasn't been a moment from the first time I've seen her that I haven't wanted her.

"You may be in charge," she says, "but you're doing it wrong."

Scowling, I lean close to her, inhaling the soft scent of orange, but shoving down the urge to move even nearer, to inhale again. Instead, I focus on what's more important. *Cookies.* "I'm not doing it wrong," I grumble, peering over her shoulder and glancing into the mixing bowl. There's butter, sugar, flour, chocolate chips, all the normal things that go into making chocolate chip cookies.

Check. Check. Check.

"Okay, sugar lips," I drawl, shifting to lean a hip against the counter. "Want to clue me into what exactly I'm doing wrong?"

She huffs out a beleaguered sigh, drops the wooden spoon into the bowl—because if Grandma taught me anything, it's that mixing by hand is the best—and cuts her gaze to the side.

Which is when I see something I hate.

Something that means she's right and I'm wrong.

Christ, I'm never going to hear the end of it.

"The batter looked wrong," she says by way of explanation, and if I hear a hint of remorse in her tone, then she must really feel sorry for me. "How many?"

"Three."

She nods but doesn't say anything else as she scoops up the carton and pulls out three eggs, making quick work of cracking them into the bowl.

I steal the bowl from her once the eggs are in and start mixing the cookie dough, loving the little sound she makes in the back of her throat.

She's frustrated with me, which is way better than the pity from the last couple of weeks, and frankly, so much better than her normal reaction to me.

That being her ignoring me.

I like her frustrated.

I love it when she can't ignore me.

Yeah, I'm an asshole.

"I can do it," she snaps, whirling toward me, reaching for the bowl.

I keep it out of her reach. "I know you can, but it's *my* job."

"Says who?"

"Seriously?"

"I could have just bought cookies from the grocery store."

"And they wouldn't be as good as mine," I say, still stirring.

She scowls.

"And because I know you love both chocolate *and* my cookies, why don't you just let me work so we all get what we want as quickly as possible?"

She huffs out a sigh, but as is often the case with Dessie, she doesn't just give in, doesn't accept defeat. She just...finds a way to bypass it. Case in point? She doesn't engage in this argument with me further, just turns away, picks up a cookie sheet from the opposite counter and brings it over, dropping it with a loud clatter.

Then immediately steals the bowl once I finish mixing and starts to spoon out the dough.

"You know," I drawl, leaning past her and fixing a lopsided ball, "one could say *you're* doing it wrong."

"Just add the salt," she grinds out, shooting a glare my direction. "I'm PMSing and need chocolate."

"So *that's* why I get the pleasure of cranky Dessie," I tease.

She just scowls at me again before she carries the bowl to the other cookie sheet and keeps scooping. "I don't know why you couldn't make these before you came over like a normal person," she mutters. "Then I wouldn't be stuck talking to you when I could be self-medicating with chocolate."

My mouth kicks up. "I didn't know you liked something about me enough to stoop low enough to endure my presence."

"I like the cookies you happen to make," she says tartly. "That doesn't mean I like *you*."

"Yeah, about that," I say, not taking her words personally—we're long past that—as I finish with the salt, lean close, and swipe my finger into the bowl, scooping up a dollop. E. coli or not, I won't turn down raw cookie dough. "You never *did* explain what your problem with me is."

"Annie—"

"Nope," I remind her. "You hated me long before that."

Her expression gentles. "I am sorry," she says. "That Annie..." She trails off and I almost feel bad for her.

"I have a great mom."

More gentle, and swear to fuck, it's like she's wrapped her hand around my cock and squeezed. I don't often get to see this side of Dessie, and it's intoxicating as hell.

"I'm luckier than Rosie in a lot of ways," I go on. "I never dealt with what she did, never had to feel like I wasn't wanted." A beat. "She deserved better."

Guilt slithers through me.

"She did," Dessie agrees.

And for a moment we exist in perfect harmony.

But her stare drifts back to mine and she lies with that gorgeous mouth. "I don't have a problem with you."

The edgy tone makes me smile.

"You *don't* have a problem with me?" I ask, not able to smother the laughter in my tone.

"Nope." Her shoulders tense.

"Are you sure?"

"Yup."

"Seriously?" I press, my temper beginning to fray at the edges. "*That's* what you're going with?"

"Fine," she snaps. "Yes, you're annoying, and everyone knows it." She rolls her eyes, picks up a cookie sheet, and carries it over to the oven. "But aside from *that*, no, I don't have a problem with you."

I laugh, watch as it makes her shoulders lift higher, the tension in her frame ratcheting even more tightly, until she resembles a coiled spring ready to explode.

"Right," I say dryly.

Her chin comes up. "I *don't.*"

"Such a beautiful liar."

A flush spreads out on her cheeks, but she just snags the other cookie sheet and shoves it into the oven. "I'm not a liar."

Ha.

This woman is full of secrets and deceptions and distance.

But...

I know her well enough by now to bite back the urge from pushing this further.

Instead, like I do on the ice—or maybe like I've learned from *her* over the last year—I pivot.

"Well," I say quietly, "if you really don't have a problem with me...then prove it."

Immediately, her head swivels, gaze snapping toward mine, mouth pressing into a firm line. "I don't need to prove anything to you." Those deep brown eyes blaze as she glowers at me.

"Hmm," I say. "Maybe that's true." I lift one shoulder with a careless shrug that I know will piss her off.

"Maaaybe?" she asks, drawing out the word with deadly intent.

Yes, *maybe,"* I say, stepping a little closer, clenching my hands into fists at my sides, desperate to touch her, to stroke the velvet of her skin, to run my fingers through the silky black locks held tight in a ponytail that teases her nape, but also knowing that she won't welcome the contact.

That if I so much as dare to lay a finger on her, my balls will be in my throat.

Her eyes are filled with fury. Her chin comes up higher. Rage sparks across her expression.

But all of that is here and gone in a second.

Furious, passionate woman is replaced with an icy, steel-covered mask.

God, I hate when she does that.

"Pray tell me," she says with a roll of her eyes, "how can I prove it to you?"

Smirking, I step a little closer, edging into the bright, citrus scent of her, the heat of her body, the need I feel when I'm close to her. "You really want to know?"

Her mouth hitches up into a sarcastic smile that has heat edging towards my dick. "Yeah, big shot." Her eyes cut south and then back up to mine, derision in their chocolate depths. "I'm positively desperate to know."

I bend, having to do it a long way because she's so much smaller than me, but not stopping until my lips are nearly at her ear.

My beard brushes against her hair.

My nose fills with her scent.

"Meet me at Maggie's"—the only halfway nice restaurant in town—"tomorrow. Seven o'clock."

She jerks and I straighten, mouth falling open. "What the fuck, Fox?"

I shrug again. "*Then* you can prove it to me."

And with her mouth gaping open, I check on the cookies, set a timer on my phone, and head out onto the porch.

Then I proceed with doing something I've become incredibly comfortable and familiar with over the last months.

Avoiding Dessie.

Even as I track her coming out a few minutes behind me.

Even at I watch her sipping her beer.

Even as I strain to hear what Bailey says that makes her laugh.

Even as...she's the first to the plate of hot cookies when I bring them out.

FOUR

DESSIE

I wipe down the bar, gaze cutting to the side, keeping a wary eye on the entrance of Monroe's.

My uncle's bar.

It's comfortable. It's home. It's...a great place to go and forget about the shitshow my life has turned into.

And really, my uncle needs me to manage it.

Monroe's is a lot for him to run on his own, and I have plenty of time on my hands and—

"You're not supposed to be working tonight," he says, his tone taking on an edge I don't love.

It means he's on to me...

And my avoidance.

"Stockroom needed a refresh," I mutter.

He pauses then leans a hip against the bar, and I nearly groan at the universal code for an incoming conversation that's sure to be long, soul-searching—at least when it comes to my uncle. His words when he speaks a moment later confirm I'm right. He's far softer than normal, "Dessie, kiddo," he says gently—fucking *gently*, "the stockroom has never been more organized"—his eyes flick to the side, toward the steel counter I've been wiping down —"and this whole space is clean enough to run a science experiment on. What's going on?"

I'm avoiding a certain location—*cough* my apartment—in case a certain hockey player shows up.

Same as I'm keeping my eye on the front door.

If I had a life, I'd go somewhere else.

Somewhere far away.

It's just...well, I have my friends.

And I have Monroe's.

Something I know that Fox *knows*, considering that I spend almost every waking moment here.

But since Bailey and company are back in the Bay Area, getting ready with their men for the upcoming Gold season, and I have absolutely no intention of going to Maggie's or being a sitting duck in my apartment...I'm hiding here.

At least the bar has two exits.

"I took a vacation not that long ago," I hedge, dropping the towel onto the counter and turning to give him my best I'm-totally-fine-and-don't-feel-like-my-life-is-falling-apart-and-that-I'm-a-giant-failure look.

One he doesn't buy given the expression he tosses back.

Oh, and the fact that he calls me out on my—

"Bullshit."

"It's not," I press on, knowing that I'll either have to argue with him—and continue to lie—or make a break from it, hole up, and hope that Fox was just fucking with me like usual.

Don't back down.

Don't *ever* back down.

The familiar mantra—the words that helped me power through a toxic work environment, that helped me when I lost my dream career, that helped me when I moved home like a fucking failure—somehow don't have the same charm they used to.

Or effectiveness.

"And remember that vacation?" I narrow my eyes when he glares at me. "Don't think I forgot the state of this place when I returned."

His cheeks, mostly hidden beneath a bushy white beard and handlebar mustache flashes red. "Managed just fine all these years without that damned computer."

"That *damned computer* houses the inventory system I implemented so you're not sending servers out to the grocery store because we're out of onions or milk."

He scowls.

And I take advantage of the fact that he's momentarily stymied to lean over, press a kiss to his cheek. "And on that note," I murmur, "I'll head home. Call me if you need anything."

His face smooths out. "Now that Rosie has taken the town's hockey players in hand"—by playing matchmaker with her niece and Axel, former ringleader of said hockey players—"there's nothing to worry about here." He pats my shoulder. "Go home, Dessie girl. Get some rest and don't even think about coming in tomorrow—"

"I—"

He fixes me with a glare that even *I* have to give in to—

Not backing down. Nope. Just...choosing my battles.

"Fine," I mutter. "But I'll be in Friday for the dinner rush. And I don't want to hear any arguments about it," I add, jabbing my finger in his direction.

He ignores me. "Dessie—"

"No." Another jab. "*Arguments.*"

A sigh. "Go on then, kid. And I'll see you Friday," he adds begrudgingly.

Damn right he will.

Because, seriously, what else do I have to do?

I keep that thought to myself as I grab my coat and purse from the office, as I delay as long as I dare taking a look through my inventory system, making sure everything's on track. But as it nears seven-thirty, I know that I need to make my escape before my uncle catches me...

Or before Fox comes in.

If, for some insane reason, he *was* serious about meeting me at Maggie's, he'll have realized by now that I'm not going to show up.

Which means...

He'll come *here*.

And the last thing I need right now is to have to deal with him in front of my uncle.

In front of half of River's Bend (the other half being down the street at Haggarty's).

I zip out the back door, turn for the staircase that leads up to my apartment—

Yes, I live above Monroe's.

No, it's not ideal for avoiding someone who might be looking for me.

I'm working with what I've got, okay?

I clutch my purse in my hand, tuck my coat beneath my arm, and run up to the second floor, my gaze swiveling from side to side.

Looking out for a certain giant, bearded, annoying as hell hockey player.

And no, I'm not disappointed when he doesn't emerge from the shadows as I run.

And I'm certainly not disappointed when I make it upstairs and he's not standing outside my door, looking to confront me for standing him up.

And I'm absolutely, definitely not disappointed when I unlock the front door, flick on the lights, and find my apartment empty, Fox not having mysteriously found a way to get inside.

Or less *mysteriously* and more...

Breaking and entering.

But there's no hockey player.

My apartment's empty.

And I'm left with...well, not disappointment, but also, perhaps, something that feels a lot like...

Disappointment.

"Dumb," I whisper, shutting the door behind me.

But...he still might show.

Which is why I lock up, turn off the lights, and sit on my couch in the dark, waiting for him to come and knock on the door until I answer (which I won't because...*don't back down. Ever.*).

But...

There's no knocking at my door.

Same as there are no calls or texts on my phone—even though I check regularly.

There's no sign of any hockey players—not even the big, annoying one who I stood up—as eight o'clock ticks by.

Then nine.

Then ten.

Which is the moment I realize I'm being dumb.

Fox was messing with me.

It's what he does. It's what *we* do.

Tease and annoy and push each other's buttons.

Of course tonight would be no different.

I drop my cell on the table in disgust (this entire scene is pathetic) and turn on the lights. It takes no time at all to get into my pajamas, to take off my makeup, to get the good snacks from the pantry.

Same as it takes no time at all to find a bad movie to watch and set it streaming.

Easy.

Without issue—or annoying hockey players.

But...

Lonely maybe.

The rest of my friends have lives, have people who love them or kids who keep them busy, or fulfilling careers.

And I...

Well, I'm back at the beginning.
Back in River's Bend.
Back working at Monroe's.
Back living in this fucking apartment.
Alone.
Again.

FIVE

FOX

I knew she wasn't going to show up, and that's why instead of heading to Maggie's at seven o'clock, I stay home and wait.

And plan.

And *wait.*

And once I'm absolutely sure that Dessie's uncle will have sent her home from the bar—because we're not doing this in the front room of Monroe's with half the fucking town looking on—I drive over to her apartment.

I pull in behind Monroe's, park in the small lot there, and look up at the second-floor railing that does little to obscure the entrance to Dessie's apartment. I'm not a fan of her living above the bar, and I like even less the fact that her front door is visible from the parking lot—and thus vulnerable—to any drunk assholes hanging out around in the dark after last call.

But that's something for another day.

Tonight I'm...

Well, I'm being a fucking idiot.

Or maybe I'm finally doing something smart, something I should have done months ago.

Something I've avoided because I was too chicken shit to risk fucking with the status quo.

But...that's done.

I'm moving, and I don't want to leave her behind.

And she...well, maybe it's purely out of pity, but this is the most open to me that she's been in years.

I need to see this through.

I've watched Axel and Bailey find their way to something damned close to perfect despite a plethora of obstacles. I've watched Billie Rose navigate a shitstorm and come through, if not unscathed, but whole, and she did it largely because she had Joel at her side.

So, the least I can do is clear the air between Dessie and me.

And maybe...I can find a way for this woman to stop glaring at me, to stop poking at me, to...

Finally move forward.

Explore the connection between us.

And the almost palpable sexual attention I feel every time I'm within a hundred feet of her?

Maybe I can do something about that too.

My dick twitches and I glare down at it, silently ordering it to behave.

Patience.

This is not about getting a taste of Dessie—not solely, not *yet*. This is about doing something different, something better, something—I reach over and snag the bag of cookies from the passenger's seat of my car—that may win over a woman's heart.

A woman who is more porcupine than soft female when it comes to me.

But one who's...

Going to be mine.

"Enough," I mutter, popping the door and unfolding myself from my sedan, careful not to hit my head because no matter how big of a car I get, I still manage to crack my skull on the frame regularly.

Tonight, though, I escape without head injury then cross the dark parking lot, climbing the stairs to Dessie's apartment. There are lights on inside, and I can hear the soft echo of a TV through the front door.

She's home.

Excellent.

Yeah, this is working exactly as I planned.

I knock.

There's a long pause, and the TV goes quiet. I don't panic, just wait, knowing she's going to be laser-focused on the door, hoping that the intruder leaves her be.

In answer to that silent glare, I just knock again.

More quiet, and for a long moment, nothing happens.

But then I hear footsteps approach the door, and my heart beats faster, my pulse picks up its pace through my veins, and my lungs work in overtime as every nerve in my body becomes completely focused on the woman walking my way.

There's a rattle as the lock is disengaged, another as the chain is pulled free, and then the door is whipped open.

"What the fuck are you doing here?" she snaps.

My anger wants to match that anger. To fight temper with temper.

I push that down.

That's not what I'm here for. Plus, I know my temper is fed by my frustration because this woman doesn't see me, doesn't like me, doesn't *want* me, even after all this time.

But I'm done with that shit.

I win on the ice.

I'm going to win off it too.

"Hey, sugar lips," I taunt, crossing my arms and leaning a shoulder back against the open door frame.

She scowls, and, fuck, she's beautiful when she does that, same as she is when she smiles, when she glowers, when she laughs, when she torments me or says my name like it's the worst curse on the planet.

Her scowl stays in place at my greeting, and she doesn't react other than to tense when I shift a little closer. "Why are you here?" she grits out.

I lift a sardonic brow. "I thought you were gonna prove it to me."

Her chin comes up. "I don't need to prove anything to you."

Grinning, I allow my asshole to peek out as I drag my gaze down her body and then back up, smile widening as her cheeks flush. "Clearly."

She's in pajamas—adorable fucking pajamas. The bottoms are dotted with hedgehogs and puffy clouds, and she's wearing a matching tank that shows off her lithe curves.

Curves I start to make a comment about.

But then I manage to tear my gaze from her tits in time to see something that turns my blood to ice.

Hurt.

Fuck.

"Dessie," I begin, remorse tearing through me.

She thinks—

Her lips press flat, the emotion gone in an instant, but just because it's buried doesn't mean it's not in her, in the tension in her shoulders, the muscle ticking in her jaw, the frost in her normally hot brown eyes. "I'm tired," she says frostily, the tone settling heavily on my shoulders and filling me with renewed guilt. "Since I'm going to go to bed without *impressing* anyone."

"Des—"

She turns away from me, reaching for the door, starting to swing it shut.

I catch it before it can latch, slip inside and close the wooden panel behind me before she can protest.

"Get out of my apartment," she snaps as I lock it.

I fucked up.

Already.

Dammit.

I grit my teeth together then exhale. "I'm sorry."

"Just go away, Fox," she mutters. "I don't need an apology. Least of all from you."

"I didn't mean it like that."

"Sure you didn't." One slender shoulder lifts then drops in a frustrated shrug. "And anyway, I just need all annoying hockey players to leave me the fuck alone."

"All?"

She crosses her arms. "*All.*"

I exhale quietly, grab tight to my temper then say, keeping my tone deliberately light, "You stood me up."

She sniffs. "Come on, you didn't actually think I was going to meet you at Maggie's."

"Maybe not." I step a little closer. "I *did* think you were going to prove that you didn't have a problem with me, though."

Her laughter is brittle. "Funny story, Fox. But I think that we're both equally guilty of having issues with each other."

I dark to tuck a strand of hair behind her ear. "Not exactly."

She lifts her brows in question.

"My only problem is that you hate me," I explain.

Only the moment the words cross my tongue, I still again.

Because it's not hurt drifting across her face this time. It's...

Guilt.

"What the fuck, Dessie?"

Her body goes ramrod stiff. Her expression locks down, even tighter than before.

"Just go away," she says quietly.

"Hey." I move closer to her, cup her jaw. "Just drop the tough girl act for once and talk to me."

She jerks out of my hold. "It's not an act."

"Dammit, sugar lips," I snap. "Just *stop*. I'm not some asshole trying to hit on you in the bar"—I'm just an asshole who wants to get in her pants—"I know you."

"You don't," she denies.

"I know you enough to see through this bullshit." I wave a

hand at her—the mask, the pulling back, the shadows in her eyes. "You've been off. What's going on?"

"Nothing."

"Is that why your friends practically had to twist your arm to get you to dinner last night?"

A flush spreads out on her cheeks. "I didn't have coverage at the bar."

"And the time before that?"

Her flush grows. "One of the servers called out late."

"And before *that?*"

"Ugh," she snaps. "Why do you care? Are you my keeper?"

"No, Des," I say. "I just pay attention."

Pay attention to everything about her.

"I'm fine."

"So fine that you decided to kill time in the kitchen last night with someone you can't stand?" I ask. "Thus avoiding any extra contact with your best friends?"

She stills. "I feel sorry for you is all."

That stings. I can't lie.

But I see it for the distraction it is. "At least I'm dealing with the bullshit from my past."

"And what? You're magically over it?"

I laugh darkly. "God no. But I'm working on it," I say. "And I'm not in denial, trying to pretend that trauma doesn't exist."

There's a long blip of quiet.

Then she mutters, "I'm tired. You need to go."

"Liar," I accuse, stepping close again, cupping her jaw, feeling the silk of her skin beneath my fingertips. "You're hiding something, sugar. Something you don't want even your friends to know."

A sharp shake of her head. "No, I'm not."

I lift my brows.

"Like I said, I'm tired."

"Okay, so say I buy that," I say, my tone clearly conveying that I don't, not at fucking all. "Then why?"

A sharp sigh. "Why what?"

"Then why"—I brush my finger along her bottom lip—"did you choose to spend time micromanaging my cookies last night?"

Her throat works, and her voice is almost inaudible when she whispers, "I don't hate you."

I open my mouth, but I don't get the chance to reply.

Because she bursts into tears.

SIX

DESSIE

Oh God.

I'm crying—something I never allow myself to do —and I'm doing it in Fox Brown's arms.

And he's not telling me to stop.

Instead, he's just wrapped his big, strong arms around me and tugged me into his body, cradling me against his chest, rubbing one broad hand gently up and down my spine. "Easy, sugar," he murmurs. "Just breathe."

That feels impossible right now—my lungs shuddering, my breaths coming in rapid gusts, my tears pouring down my cheeks.

I buried this all so long ago, and I don't know why it's coming out now.

And, worst of all, why it's coming out with Fox, the man who lives to torment me.

No, that's not fair.

He's the man who pushes my buttons as much as I push his.

Because from the first time I saw him, I wanted him.

And if I've learned anything over the last years is that if I want a man, he's destined to break my heart.

Case in point?

My high school boyfriend dumped me for the head cheerleader the night before prom.

And my college boyfriend, well, he left me because he found his "soulmate"...who happened to be my *room*mate.

Not to mention that my dating experiences as an adult have been littered with matches on apps and failed dates (including one where the man I was interested took me to dinner the left me with a big-ass bill because he was *hungry* and another who tried to get me to play a DoorDash driver by picking up dinner—and paying for it—then driving it out to his place because he didn't have a car).

Winners.

I always picked winners.

And there was Jett. The man I dated before moving home to River's Bend. The man who proposed to me, who I was so excited to spend the rest of my life with—so much so that I was willing to leave my job for him.

Only to find out he was cheating on me.

And *when* did I find out?

The same night I accepted his ring.

Ugh.

Jett was an asshole—I know that now, understand it, especially after seeing how Axel and Joel interact with Bailey and Billie Rose, after seeing my best friends so happy and in love.

I wasn't like that with Jett.

I wasn't...*me*.

I was smaller, quieter...diminished.

And he certainly didn't adore me in the same way the guys love my best friends.

My throat burns, and I know I should lift my head, should pull away from Fox. Should shove this all down and keep pushing forward.

Don't back down.

But...I'm tired.

And there's something wrong with me, something broken with my "picker."

All of which to say—

I know—*fucking* know—by now that if I want a man, that's the clearest signal to me to run the fuck away.

And if I *can't* run?

Then it's time to put up as many barriers as possible, bricks and barbed wire and bombs that will detonate to keep the danger at a distance.

Like a cornered dog growling to get someone to leave it alone.

Normally it works—far too well.

But, just now, when Fox looked at my body and—

Dammit.

That look of derision.

It's so fucking familiar.

Jett perfected it.

My other boyfriends tried it.

And I...well, I tried to logic my way through it.

But...

It still hurts.

I'll never be slender and petite like Bailey. Nor a curvy dynamo like Rosie. I'm tall with broad shoulders and muscular biceps, and I can dead lift more than most of the guys at the gym I attend.

And Fox's look brought that all up again—the vulnerability, the need, the...

Loneliness.

Knowing I'll never find someone to love me for me. Not really.

Ugh. Why didn't he just leave when I asked?

Then he would have never seen me like this, and I could go back to pretending to hate him, spending all my spare energy turning Monroe's into the best bar on the planet, and being happy for my friends and how wonderful their lives have turned out.

This, though?

This I can't undo.

He's seen behind the veil, and if I know anything about Fox it's that he's not the kind of man to let this go.

Stubborn.

Pushy.

Damn.

I tremble and he murmurs, "Easy," again, still rubbing my back with that big hand, still holding me gently even though, looking at him, there should be nothing gentle about the huge hockey player. He's so tall that I feel small, so strong and built that when I'm pressed against him, I feel delicate and feminine.

And for a woman whose dream it was to spend her life *saving* lives in between hauling hoses, using axes to break down walls, carrying gear and oxygen tanks and the occasional unconscious body out of buildings, feeling small and delicate and feminine...

Is not common.

That Fox manages to invoke those feelings just while holding me in the hallway of my apartment when he doesn't really like me, when we're always picking at each other...

It's not the Fox I know.

Not the Fox who's always prepped with a joke, who loves kids, who cares deeply about my friends just because they love *his* people—and who've become his people now too.

And not just because Rosie's his half-sister.

I always knew Fox Brown was dangerous to me—hence the barbed wire and brick walls and big ass bombs—but in *this* moment, with his arms around me?

I've never realized anything is more true.

Wrapped in his embrace, smelling his spicy, male scent, feeling his body pressed to mine...makes me want so much more than I know I can have.

Makes me want so much more than I would ever allow myself to even think I *could* have again.

But I still can't make myself step away.

Can't pull out of his hold, can't drag myself from the heat of his body, the scent of him in my nose. Can't bring myself to stop him from murmuring gentle words at me, from soaking in the comfort he's offering.

Only...when he leans back and swipes a thumb beneath one of my eyes and then the other, gently brushing my tears away, I know I *have* to.

Have to go cold turkey before I get addicted and deal with withdrawal from the drug known as Fox.

But even as I gather my defenses, as I prepare to erect them between this man and my heart, I get a glimpse of his face.

And yep, I know I've ruined everything.

Panic slices through me.

"You should go," I say quickly, jerking out of his hold and rushing to the front door.

I wrap my fingers around the metal handle, but before I can turn the knob, he's there, his chest against my back, his body surrounding mine, his palm settling on my hand.

"Don't," he whispers.

"I can't do this," I whisper back.

His fingers flex around mine, but the rest of his body grows still. "Sugar."

"You should just go."

He shifts a little closer, and my eyes slide closed at the feel of him. "You won't tell me?"

God, I want to, especially when he uses that soft voice to gentle me, when he's so close, when he's being so, *so* careful with his strength.

But—as previously explained—my picker is broken.

I'm broken.

And I want him too much to risk letting him in.

"I'm fine," I lie.

"You just spent the last twenty minutes crying in my arms, baby."

My heart squeezes hard. "I told you I was PMSing."

He's quiet and statue still for a long, *long* moment.

Then he exhales and the blip of guilt I feel when I hear the disappointment in his voice cuts deep. "Okay, sugar," he says quietly. "I'll go home, even though you didn't give a second thought to standing me up."

And...cue more guilt.

"Fox—" I begin.

He lets his hand drop, steps back, and stomach twisting, I turn to face him.

"I'm sor—" But my words cut off because the moment I see his face, I realize I've been had.

Jesus, he's laying it on thick.

"Just go," I mutter.

His beautiful brown eyes are dancing—clearly recognizing that I've picked up on his shenanigans. He holds up a bag. "But if you kick me out, I'll keep these for myself."

My stomach rumbles.

That zip top bag is full of his cookies.

The best fucking chocolate chip cookies on the planet.

"Seriously?" I glare. "You're going to tease me like that?"

A wicked smile. "Oh no, sugar. I never tease."

I shiver, his words stroking like fingers between my legs. "Fox," I warn.

His smile just widens, and he shakes the bag. "So, you going to tell me why you don't like me?"

"That's easy," I grumble, reaching for the bag, which, annoyingly, he sweeps out of reach, "because you won't share the cookies."

"*Pft.* That's not the only reason."

Ugh.

I clamp my lips together, reach for the bag again.

He chuckles. "Thought so. Well then"—a nod to the door—"I'll just take my treats and leave."

"Fine." Scowling, I start to step back.

He reaches for the handle, stops. "Unless...."

Right. I'm this close to pushing a certain hockey player over the second story railing. "Just go, Fox."

"Unless...you want to *share* the cookies," he offers.

My temple throbs. "And what do *you* get in exchange in this arrangement?"

There's a long pause, the tension in the room seeming to ratchet up before he grins again. "Got any beer?"

And *that's* how—*somehow*—I end up spending the night with the man I hate the most.

Or maybe that's how—*somehow*—I finally start coming back to myself.

SEVEN

Fox

"You know," she says, the words slightly slurred, several hours later, "I don't hate you."

We're on the second bad movie—because the crazy woman apparently likes to watch movies with plots that make no fucking sense.

Case in point?

We're watching a film about a troll inhabiting an apartment building in San Francisco...and it's not a kids' movie. This being after I sat on the couch, exchanged a handful of cookies for a bottle of beer, and watched the tail end of a movie about sharks who can somehow "swim" in the sand on beaches.

Yup. It makes no sense.

But I got to watch Dessie cackle and hoard the cookies I passed her like she was Gollum with the ring that ruled them all, and...

Drink beer.

Until the tension began to leave her body and she stopped looking over at me every few seconds as though she expected me to turn and attack.

Chocolate, sugar, and beer.

And bad movies.

They tame the beast that is Dessie.

Noted.

"I don't hate you either," I tell her, offering up the last cookie in the bag.

She exhales. "So why do we put so much effort into pretending we do?"

"I don't know," I admit, head buzzing from the beers I drank and tongue suitably loosened enough to add, "Except that it seems like sometimes when you're pissed at me it's the only time you actually see me."

Her inhale is sharp. "I—" A shaky exhale. "Seriously?" she whispers.

I shrug. "I walked into Monroe's that first night, and it was like you hated me on sight."

"You came with the reputation of the Rush Hockey squad."

"For the record, I was never into the whole property damage side those losers seemed to revel in."

"Just the carousing and women and being general nuisances?" she asks drolly.

My lips twitch. "You know me, sugar lips. Do I enjoy being a nuisance?"

Not even a second of hesitation when she says, "Yes."

Our eyes connect and then we both start busting up, the sounds of the trolls growling on the TV echoing through the room behind us. But I'm barely aware of the wizardly battle taking place in the background.

All I see is Dessie.

Her smile wide, her eyes dancing, her expression relaxed. She's not like this with me, not ever. Even when she's ignoring me, there's tension around her mouth, in her shoulders.

"So, nuisance tendencies aside, why do you really not like spending time with me?" I blurt.

I know the moment I ask the question that it's a mistake.

Then tension roars back in an instant.

"Sugar," I say, "ignore me."

"No," she whispers, and I hate that she seems small right now, that my words reduced her from the bright, beautiful woman to...

This.

"It's okay," I say. "I'm an idiot. Let's just watch the movie and—"

"I'm attracted to you."

My mouth drops open, and I sputter for a few long moments. "Um, is this a problem?"

Her cheeks turn red, and she groans. "Oh my God," she mutters, dropping her face into her hands. "I did *not* fucking admit that."

"Sugar—"

"No," she snaps, head shooting up, eyes narrowed into a glare. "*Don't.*"

I lean over, ignoring when she tenses further, when she starts to shift away from me. "You're the most beautiful woman I've ever seen," I rasp, cupping her face in both of my hands. "I've dreamed about you every fucking night from the first time I saw you at Monroe's."

She shakes her head. "That's not. *No.*" She pulls back, and this time, I let her go because...

Of course I do.

I have to.

But I don't give up. "Is that so hard to believe?"

"Yes."

"Dessie, baby, you have to know how gorgeous you are."

She snorts, but before I can push that, she says, "So, you're what"—her lips press flat—"just a little boy pulling on my braid because you *like* me?"

"Yes." I lift a shoulder, drop it carelessly. "And if I had a frog, I'd put it in your desk."

She scowls.

"It's the same principle as you always making sure my beer is more foam than alcohol when I come into Monroe's and you're on shift."

Her eyes slide away, but I don't miss the flush spreading out over her cheeks. "I—"

Moving close, I cup her jaw again. "I don't mind that. Fuck, you could never serve me a beer again and it would be fine. It...it only really hurts when you ignore me."

"Dammit," she whispers, her shoulders slumping. "This isn't a good idea."

"Finally putting our cards on the table?"

"Yes, it's a fucking terrible decision."

"I—" Then I blink, the rest of my words stoppered up in the back of my throat as she stands and takes a couple of quick steps away from the table.

"Sugar?"

"*No.*"

"Dessie—"

"I'm broken," she says, turning away from me, her black ponytail swinging behind her. "It's inevitable that this will all just blow up in my face and then where will I go? I don't have fire-fighting anymore. If don't have Monroe's or River's Bend or Rosie or Bailey—"

"Why would you lose your friends or River's Bend, sugar?" I ask gently, moving toward her.

Those shoulders hitch up again and I expect her to ignore me, to lie, to come up with some bullshit excuse to put me off.

But...

She doesn't.

Instead she turns to me and whispers, "Because that's what always happens. With men. With people I think are my friends. With my job. With—"

Her voice cracks, and I take a half step forward, prepared to cradle her close again, prepared to wipe her tears away.

"Des," I whisper.

"I hate you because I want you," she says. "Because every

single time I allow my heart to make the decision to overrule my mind, I end up bruised and battered and alone. I can't have that happen. Not again."

Shit.

My heart aches, and my anger ramps.

I want to hold her again, and I want to demand that she explain herself, that she give me the name of every single person who hurt her.

But I need to know the rest of it.

"Is that why you came back to River's Bend?" I ask carefully. "Because people you cared about hurt you?"

"People I cared about." She sighs and spins back to face me, eyes widening as though not realizing I had come so close. But she just side-steps me, moves to the table, and picks up the last beer, chugging down a large sip of it. "Yes," she whispers. "My fiancé and my coworker he was fucking."

I frown. "But weren't you working at—"

"The station?" she finishes, and I nod. "Yup. Turns out it's not all that hard to cheat when your partner is working long hours and away from home days on end." A sigh as she takes another long drag on the bottle. "But Jett isn't the only asshole to break my heart. I'm not good at this, Fox. Not good at picking people who will be good for me."

"So what?" I ask. "You're just going to hole up and hide from life?"

Her brows drag together, tone going deadly. "Excuse me?"

But really? She's going to be a coward?

Dessie?

"You're scared, sugar lips," I tell her. "Scared of getting hurt again, but"—I shrug—"that's fucking life. Things don't work out, we date people who are bad for us. We hide from the truth" —fuck, do I know *that*—"but if we're just hiding from everything that might hurt us then we might as well not—"

"What?" she asks when I don't finish. "Might as well not *what?*"

I sigh. "You know what I mean."

"Tell me," she grits out.

"Fine," I say. "You really want to do this?"

She waves a hand around her apartment. "I think *you're* the one doing this, hot shot. *You* showed up at my door. *You* hung around. *You* wanted to know the truth. And *you're* the one pushing *this* right now."

"Maybe I *am* the one pushing this." I move over to her. "But I'm also not the one hiding."

Not hiding *this*.

I touch her cheek. "I've had my heart broken. More than once. I've been cut from teams I was desperate to play for. And up until a couple weeks ago, I thought I was never going to make it to my end goal. But, fuck, sugar, we have one life to live." I drop my hands onto her shoulders. "Is this"—I glance around the room—"living alone, too scared to go after what you desire really *all* you want from yours?"

EIGHT

DESSIE

The disappointment in Fox's eyes when he left last night is almost impossible to shake.

What's worse?

The disappointment I feel in myself because I answered his question with the affirmative.

Is this living alone, too scared to go after what you desire really all you want from yours?

And I'd said...

Yes.

"Ugh," I mutter, lifting the lid of the dumpster and tossing the bag of trash inside.

The beer bottles clink and I feel another twinge of guilt.

Sleep was a long time coming after listening to the *click* of the front door closing, to Fox's muffled voice through the wooden panel ordering me to lock up.

I had done just that, flicking the lever, securing the chain, but my mind had been strangely blank.

Same as it had been when I crossed the room and sank onto the couch. As it had been when I watched the end of the movie—

and why there's no way I can tell anyone how the troll was vanquished because while my gaze was trained on the TV's screen, I wasn't absorbing a damned thing.

Because all I could think—*can* think—is—

All you want from yours?

Once upon a time I'd wanted everything.

Now...I know better.

"Enough." I exhale and turn for the bar, intending to find some task inside Monroe's to keep me busy, but the moment I get close to the back door, I see my uncle standing there. Beard bushy, eyes tired, arms crossed.

"I told you not until Friday."

"I know," I mutter, trying to shift around him, to sneak my way inside. "I just need—"

"Turn around, Dessie girl."

"Uncle Roger," I say, exasperated. "I got a full night's rest"—*ha*—"and you didn't. Let me get a bit ahead for you today so—"

He pushes off the door, crosses to me, and grips the tops of my shoulders, giving me a light shove in the direction of the parking lot. "Go out, get a cup of coffee with your friends, take a walk, touch some fucking grass or something. Just don't keep hanging around here."

"I like it here," I protest, shrugging off his hold and spinning to face him.

It's home.

It's comfortable.

More importantly, it's safe.

"Honey," he says on a sigh, wrapping his arm around my shoulders now and guiding—*read: corralling*—me toward the parking lot.

My stomach starts twisting.

I don't like the way he says that, don't like the thread of finality in his tone.

"What are you saying?" I rasp.

"I've let this go on far too long," he says, drawing up next to my car and tugging at the handle, which unlocks because, unfortunately, he has my purse in his hand and my keys are inside and that means the doors automatically unlock when he pulls, and—

"Let what go on for too long?" I ask, focusing on anything except the mess that is my head.

Sighing, he settles his hand on my shoulder again, presses down until I'm sitting in the driver's seat. "You working at the bar."

That twisting from before?

Well, it's a fucking tornado now, whipping around and around in my stomach until I feel like I might puke. "What are you saying?"

"You needed a safe place to land," he says. "But you're hiding now, Dessie girl. And I can't let you keep doing that."

Pain spears through me. "What are you saying?" I ask again.

"You can't keep working here, honey. You need to get back out there and start living again."

"I—"

He cups my jaw for a second before he leans back and reaches for my legs, tucking them into my car, tosses my purse onto the passenger's seat and says,

"You're fired."

And then he closes the door.

And walks away.

———

I don't know how I ended up in the parking lot of the coffee shop on Main Street.

Maybe it's because my uncle implanted the thought in my subconscious.

Maybe it's because it's only a couple of blocks down the road.

Maybe it's...

Pure chance.

Regardless, I'm sitting in my car, completely unaware of my

surroundings, when there's the knock on my window that snaps me out of my haze.

I jerk my head to the side, see Fox's beard first, then the concerned expression on his face when he crouches to look fully in through my window. Before I can pull myself together, he's reaching for the door handle, tugged the metal panel open. "Sugar lips," he asks, leaning into my space, inundating me with the heat of his body and his scent and all that is...

Fox.

"What's the matter, baby?" he asks.

Heart aching, I look away. "Nothing. I'm fine."

A sigh as he settles back on his haunches, one hand dropping to my knee.

The sensation brands me through my clothes, as though he's touching my naked skin.

"Liar."

I lift my chin. "Why do you always accuse me of lying?"

"Because you use your lies like a shield, sugar. And because," he adds before I can protest that, "you've been sitting here for twenty minutes staring off into space."

At that, the fight washes right out of me.

"Roger fired me," I whisper.

That wipes the self-satisfied smile off his face, but he doesn't hesitate, just reaches in, unbuckles my seat belt.

"Wh—"

He snags my arm, my purse, and then I'm out of the car, the cool morning breeze kissing my cheeks.

"What are you doing?" I ask as he closes the door, locks my car, and starts hauling me forward. I try to drag my feet, but there's no stopping his strength as he hauls me out of the parking lot and toward the huge park that takes up a large chunk of the area just off Main Street.

It houses the Rec Center. And the soccer fields. Plays host to the farmer's market on Saturdays. And it's key to the numerous festivals the town puts on—including the annual Sip and Slide wine tasting event that had taken place last weekend.

And now...me—being dragged along by an overgrown hockey player.

"Hey," I growl. "Let me go."

"Here," he mutters in response—*not* letting me go, for the record—but shoving a to go cup from the coffee shop in my hand. "Drink this," he orders.

"Let. Me. *Go.*"

"It's your favorite," he says. "A vanilla mocha with cinnamon and oat milk."

"I—"

He knows what I drink?

"I know everything about you," he murmurs, stepping closer, until I'm surrounded in his warmth again. "I'm obsessed."

"Fox," I whisper.

He stops us next to a bench, sits and draws me down next to him. "Tell me."

An order.

I should refuse on principle.

But...I can't.

"What's to tell?" I say miserably. "Roger's done with my bullshit and now I don't have a job again and—" *Christ.* My eyes begin to burn, and I almost start crying. For the second time in as many days.

Pathetic.

"Roger loves you." Fox tips the bottom of my cup up slightly, reminding me to drink my coffee while it's still hot.

Another order—albeit, a silent one.

I wrinkle my nose, but...it's coffee, so I drink.

Mostly so I don't start crying again.

"You think he doesn't?" he asks.

I avoid the question. "Is this what making peace with each other is? Coffee and me bitching about my life?"

Silence.

Nothing more than the sound of the wind in the trees, the cars slowly driving by on Main Street, the barely audible yells of the kids having a great time on the nearby playground.

"It's less bitching and more about having someone to confide in," he says. "Instead of hiding at work." He fixes me with a look. "Which, for the record, I think is what Roger's move was about this morning."

Considering that my uncle had said much the same thing—telling me to get a life and stop hiding—I can't bring myself to argue.

Not when I want to be miserable.

"I'll be fine."

Fox snorts.

"I will be."

"Is that why you were playing zombie in the parking lot?" he asks. "Why you fell apart in my arms last night?"

"I—"

"Is that why you push everyone away before they can get close?"

"Bailey and Rosie—"

"Do they know what you told me last night?" he asks gently, and he rushes to my cheeks. "No," he says with a shake of his head. "I thought so."

"They're busy," I hedge. "Bailey is still rebuilding after the fire and figuring out her life with Axel, Veronica, and Alex. And Rosie's dealing with more than enough"—the legal tangle that cost her the mayoral position and nearly her freedom—"all while falling in love. They don't need to more on their plate, especially when my stuff—"

"What?" He turns on the bench, resting an arm along the back. "When your stuff is *what*?"

"Isn't that big of a deal."

NINE

Fox

I bust up laughing.

I know it's a dick move, but I find that I can't stop myself.

She glares at me then huffs out a breath and goes back to sucking down that mocha. "It's *not* a big deal," she says again.

"Want to dig out you phone, call them, and ask?"

Her glare intensifies.

"Exactly," I say. "You know it *is* a big deal and that they'd feel the same way as I do. So," I say, exhaling and giving in to the clawing need inside me—just a little bit—by sliding closer, near enough that my knee brushes the outside of her thigh—"why don't you tell me?"

"You?"

The befuddlement on her face would be an insult if she weren't so fucking cute. "Yes. *Me.* I know about the cheating asshole." Pain darts across her face, and *I* feel like the asshole, but I stay the course, shifting nearer and tucking a strand of hair behind her ear. "Tell me what other secrets you're keeping?" I ask softly.

I know I have no right.

I haven't earned it yet.

Haven't gained her trust.

But Dessie needs me to be here listening.

"Talk to me, sugar," I press.

She's quiet for so long that I open my mouth, start to ask her again, but then she sighs, sets the cup of coffee aside, and begins to talk to me.

Without slurred words and booze in both of our systems, she tells me more about the ex who made her position at the fire station so uncomfortable that she eventually quit and moved home. And about the men before. The dick of a college boyfriend, the similarly pitiful high school one.

"So," she says quietly, her gaze trained on the trees in the distance, "like I told you last night. My picker is broken. If I'm attracted to a man, if I *want* one then I know that the smartest thing I can do is stay the hell away."

"Or make it so they stay away from you," I murmur, finally getting it now.

Another deep sigh. Then a nod. "Yeah."

"And what else?"

She looks up at me, and I know they shouldn't, but my lips turn up.

She's annoyed and she's fucking adorable when her temper is piqued.

Hell, she's fucking adorable all the time.

"How do you know there's something else?" Her voice is edgy.

I tug that strand of hair again. "Because I know you."

"How?" she asks miserably. "I swear *I* don't know who I am anymore."

That wraps a capable feminine hand around my heart and squeezes tightly. "What do you mean, sugar?"

A long, despondent exhale. "I thought I was supposed to be a firefighter and I loved it, but then I didn't." Her eyes come to mine for a blip before dancing away again. "And then I thought

Monroe's was going to be my place, but that can't be now either, I guess, and—" Her voice breaks. "Honestly? What the fuck am I doing with my life? I'm too scared to act on my feelings, I don't have a job—not even in the family business any longer—and I'm hiding from my friends and..."

"You're spinning."

She looks up at me with such consternation that I laugh. Then I do what I do best. I wrap her in my special brand of Fox Brown charm—

A hug.

"Dammit," she mutters a long moment later.

"What?" I whisper into her hair.

Oranges and woman and *mine*.

But patience now.

Go slowly so I don't spook her now that I'm through those outer layers of shields.

"I hate that you give good Hug," she mutters.

Smirking, I hold her a little tighter. "That's one of the Fox Brown superpowers, sugar lips." I tease, cupping the tops of her shoulders and leaning back so I can see her face. "Want to know what else is?"

Her nose wrinkles again, and I want to kiss the little ridges, want to just kiss *her*. "I think I should refuse to answer that, just on principle."

"But you're not going to?"

She shakes her head, sighs again. "No." It's a grumble. "So fine. Tell me what else is in your superpower wheelhouse."

I wink. "Problem solving."

————

After a workout that left my legs shaking and my abs burning, I knock on Dessie's door with my free hand.

My other being full of takeout.

Carbs. Wine. And helping her sort out her life.

That's on the agenda tonight.

And maybe also getting more of my fill of her, my drug that's Dessie—especially now that I've navigated my way through the prickly exterior.

Or maybe not, I think as I see the scowl on her face.

"What?" I ask, stepping inside when she pulls the door wide. "You don't like Italian?"

"I love it," she grumbles. "As you know," she adds, taking the bag from me, walking into the kitchen, and pulling the contents from inside, setting them onto the counter. "Considering you brought fettuccine Alfredo for me."

I *do* know this.

I know her favorite coffee, her favorite type of pasta, her favorite dessert (and yes, my ego loves that the answer to the last one is my cookies).

"So why the grumpy face?" I ask.

She pulls two beers from her fridge and plunks them onto the table. "I don't know what the hell I'm doing." She tosses her hands up. "And I think that Roger's serious! He wouldn't even let me walk into the back office. *And* he handed me my *last check.*"

Damn. Her uncle's playing hard ball.

Though, I have no doubt he'll break soon enough.

Dessie's too good at managing the bar, loves it too much for him to keep her out of it permanently.

In the meantime, it's about implementing my superpowers. "I take it that sitting around and thinking about what you want with your future didn't go well?"

The look she shoots me should eviscerate me.

I just smile and tap her nose. "Fucking adorable." Then freeze when her expression grows sad. "What is it, sugar lips?"

She sighs, cuts her gaze to the side. "If I pretend not to know will you leave me alone?"

But before I can answer that, she does.

"No," she mutters, "of course you won't." A grimace. "Because you've decided that I'm your project."

No, I've decided she's *mine*.

Not a project. Not a friend. Not a woman I care about.

M.I.N.E. *Mine.*

She just doesn't know it yet.

I grin, draw her in for a hug, and fuck if I don't fall even deeper for her when she doesn't pull away, when she just melts against my chest, lets me hold her, and sighs. "I don't know what I'm doing."

"Not working at Monroe's?"

She stiffens and glares up at me.

"Too soon?" I tease, testing the waters and pressing a kiss to her forehead.

"Definitely," she grumbles. "But also"—a sigh—"you're not wrong. It's not—" A shake of her head. "I like helping my uncle and I love most everyone in town. River's Bend is a special place. I just..."

"Want something more."

Her eyes flick to mine and there's a familiar feeling in them, one that calls to my soul. "Yes."

"I dreamed of making it to the NHL—and I did make it, for a few games, anyway. But...not how I thought it would be, and it didn't feel like I'd hoped and...fuck, just thinking about what I was going to do when my contract was up in a couple of years..."

"What?"

"It gave me hives and yet this new contract feels..." She settles her hand on my chest, just over my heart, and it allows the words to slide from my tongue. "Like I don't know what I'm doing."

"Fox," she murmurs.

"I know what I'm doing with the Rush, but the game in the NHL is faster, smarter, and..."

"You're not sure you'll be able to hang?"

I want to lie, but how the hell can I expect her to confide in me if I don't do the same?

"Yeah," I say. "Exactly that."

"Seriously?" She starts laughing.

I rock back on my heels and stare at her, mouth agape. "Something you find funny about me being vulnerable, sugar lips?"

Her mouth quirks. "Yup."

I fix her in place with my best glare. "Yup?" I repeat with deadly intent.

"Yup," she says again, those fingers on my chest flexing. "I think it's hilarious that you, Fox freaking Brown, are worried that you won't do well."

I start to reply but she just rises on tiptoe, cups the sides of my face, keeps talking.

"You're an incredible player." Her tone has my heart pulsing. "You dominated last season, did well in all of the games you played for the Gold. Yeah, the competition is going to get harder, but you're good, honey. *Really* good. And I know you'll put in the hard work to be successful."

"Christ, you're sweet," I rasp, rubbing a hand over the ache.

Those beautiful brown eyes dance. "Is that why you call me sugar?"

"Sugar *lips*," I correct gently, leaning close and tapping a finger to the offending body part. "Mostly because I've been obsessed with tasting this mouth for years now."

She inhales, and I know it would be so easy to kiss her, to finally taste her.

But...patience.

Trust.

Connection.

Mine.

I peel her hands from my cheek, press a kiss to each of her palms. Then step back, pass her a fork, and nudge her over the couch. "Eat before it gets cold, sugar lips."

She takes the container.

"And maybe you'll let me get a taste at some point."

Her mouth drops open.

Okay so that's decidedly *not* patience but also...

A little nudge forward.

Or leap.

Meh. Po-tay-to. Po-tah-to.

It's fine.

Especially since she doesn't immediately turn me down.

But...it's also a nudge I pair with pasta *and* a distraction that I drop into her lap.

Literally into her lap.

TEN

DESSIE

"No," I say on a sigh, tossing the binder of job suggestions he put together. "I will *not* be a stripper."

He tosses that wolfish grin in my direction. "But you already have experience with poles."

I roll my eyes.

But I'm secretly touched.

The man actually put together a collection of career suggestions for me.

Which is just...

Maybe the nicest thing anyone has ever done for me.

"I believe I suggested an *exotic dancer*," he says, waggling his brows. "And why not? You're hot and would be good at it."

"For one," I counter, "despite my *pole experience,* I have no rhythm. And for another, I don't think my body type"—I wave a hand down my front—"screams stripper."

The way his brows drag together in outrage may be even nicer than the whole binder of jobs. "Have you not *seen* that gorgeous body in the mirror?"

I laugh. "Oh, I've seen it. And so have my exes. I know exactly where I'm lacking—"

I barely finish the word before I find myself pinned between a hard body and the couch.

"Fox," I whisper.

Hot brown eyes on mine. "You are *not* lacking." His mouth comes so close to mine that I think he's going to kiss me.

Or maybe it's just that I'm desperate for him to slant his mouth over mine.

Instead, I only feel his words on my lips. "Not lacking in *anything*, sugar."

"Fox," I whisper again.

"This body"—a hand drags along my side—"these curves. This strength. This ass—" He groans as he palms it. "You have no idea how much I dreamed of it."

My hands tremble.

Hell, *every* part of me trembles.

I shift, spreading my legs slightly, feeling—

Oh.

That's nice.

And big.

And *nice.*

But even as I'm processing the hard length of his erection against my thigh, reveling in the pleasure of his weight pressing me into the cushions, even as I'm trying to summon the courage to part my legs a bit further and allow him even closer, he's pushing off me, sitting us both up again, saying, "So if not an exotic dancer—"

I huff out a breath and roll my eyes, but I can't fight my smile.

Each of his "suggestions" has grown increasingly more and more outrageous, and I know it's because he's trying to help me—by both making me laugh and also to see if anything resonates.

"—definitely *not* an exotic dancer."

He gives a beleaguered side that I don't buy for a second as he continues, ticking off on his fingers as he says, "We've already turned down teacher and financial analyst."

I nod.

"And park ranger and city planner and restaurant owner and"—he shakes his head at me, hang dog expression fully in place—"you also, for some reason, don't want to get rich and own a hockey team." Another beleaguered sigh. "So really, what's left now?"

It's my turn to sport that long-suffering expression.

Only mine isn't fake.

None of what he's saying, none of what he's gathered—which, as I've established is the nicest thing anyone has ever done for me—

None of them *fit*.

"Ugh," I groan, rubbing my hands over my face. "What's wrong with me?"

Suddenly, his face is in mine again, those big brown eyes filled with determination. "Do I have to talk about that ass again?"

Somehow, I laugh. "*Fox.*"

He settles his hand on the side of my neck. Gently. And I feel another piece of that shield around my heart shudder and break off. "Nothing's wrong with you, sugar," he says softly. "We'll figure something out."

My breath catches, hope blooming in my belly.

I always knew men could act like this, could *be* like this—hell, I've seen it with my friends. I just...never thought it was something *I* could have.

The gentle, the soft. The *knowing*—that something was eating me alive, that I was feeling insecure a couple of minutes ago, hell, even the fact that Fox remembered my favorite type of pasta and how I take my coffee is almost unfathomable.

Except...it's not.

Because he *did* remember. And he's here, brainstorming job ideas after having put together a color-coded—freaking *color-*

coded!—binder of options, all of which was after having brought me dinner.

And coffee.

And cookies.

And...

He's full of life, blazing bright and beautiful...

And he's here for *me*.

More pieces of my shield falling away.

Especially when he slides closer to me on the couch and slips his arm around my shoulders, tucking me into his side, sheltering me against the warmth of him. Pressed against all of that big, hard strength is quickly becoming my favorite place to be, quickly filling my dreams, taking over my fantasies.

"It'll be okay," he murmurs, tightening that arm, bringing me closer. "I promise."

I want to stay there, flush against him, but know I can't, so I push gently against his side and remind him, "You have to leave for San Jose in the morning, and you have practices, workouts, along with training camp coming up. Then the season will be here, and you'll be busy. You can't spend all of your time trying to help me fix my disaster of a life."

He lifts one of those big, strong shoulders and drops it in a careless shrug. "What else have I got to do?"

"Um," I say. "Hockey and a life that doesn't involve holding my hand?"

"Hockey's not everything."

"It's your life. Your dream."

"I don't know if you've picked up on it, but—" He laces his fingers through mine. "I kind of like this, sugar." A kiss to my knuckles. "Being here with you. Laughing and touching and talking with you."

"Fox," I murmur.

A wink. "Most especially when we're talking about your pole skills."

I swat at his shoulder. "There are no pole skills to speak of. The station didn't even have one."

His mouth curves up, making his beard twitch. "Well, that's disappointing."

"*So* disappointing," I tease. "And most of our call outs were for medical emergencies, not to actually put out fires."

"Also disappointing."

I roll my eyes. "All of that being said, you really should head home. It's late, and you have a long drive in the morning."

He turns and, if I'm not mistaken, there might be the barest thread of hurt in his eyes. You really want me to go?" he asks quietly.

Yes.

No.

Yes.

No.

But I don't say those things aloud. Instead, I remind him, "It's late and you have a life to get back to."

"Sugar."

It's a reprimand.

One I narrow my eyes at.

"Princess," I say pulling out a nickname from months ago that I know pisses him off.

But tonight, he just grins, as though it doesn't bother him in the least and says, "Trying to make me mad, sugar?"

Ugh.

Why can he read me so easily?

"I'm trying to let you off the hook," I grumble.

"And have I not made it clear that I don't want to be let *off the hook?*" he counters, turning to fully face me.

The heat in his eyes has my pulse picking up its pace, and I suck in a breath when he comes closer. The intensity woven into his expression, the coiled strength in his big body...

I want.

So fucking badly.

My thighs tremble when he settles his hand on my knee, the warmth of his palm soaking through my pants, burning into my skin.

What I wouldn't give for him to slide that hand a little higher. Then higher until—

"Have I not made it clear that I'm interested in you?" he asks, voice like roughened velvet stroking between my thighs. "Have I not made it clear that I dream about you, that I want to stroke every inch of your body, that I want to lick you from head to toe and then back up again. I need to find out how you taste, *have* to hear the sounds you make when you come. But first—" His voice drops, turning silken as he brushes his thumb along my bottom lip. "I'm just fucking desperate to kiss you."

I shiver as he nudges me back onto the cushions again, his big body coming over me, covering me from head to toe. Heat gathers between my legs, making me go damp and warm and soft.

"This is a bad idea." But I don't push him away, and my words lack any kind of strength.

"No," he says, "I think it's the best idea either of us has ever had."

I hitch my leg around his waist, feel the hard length of his erection against my pussy, and—

Yes.

That's good.

It's fucking great.

And I'm in total agreement as he groans, one hand settling at my shoulder, the thumb on the other brushing along my bottom lip again, back and forth, *back and forth.*

"I want to kiss to you," he rasps.

Heat blazes through me, erasing my common sense. "Then why aren't you?"

He settles his forehead against mine and sighs. "Because you don't trust me, sugar. And I get it. I'm not going to hurt you, but you don't believe that—"

"I want to," I whisper.

"I know," he says gently. "But you have good reason to be gun-shy." A sigh as he shifts back enough to press his lips to my forehead before rolling us to our sides, his body behind mine, his arms wrapping around me. "So back to this job thing. Tomorrow I'll—"

"You're *leaving* tomorrow," I remind him.

"And there are these things called cell phones," he teases. "Along with the internet. I won't know any of the guys on the team, and the schedule will be light at first. I'll have plenty of time to scroll through those new job listings. Plus"—he squeezes me a little tighter—"you'll only be a couple hours' drive away. I'll come up and visit. I might even"—he drops his head, inhales deeply—"bring you some cookies if you let me in."

My heart rolls over in my chest, and...I feel it then.

The last pieces of my shield fluttering away.

I've been wavering on knife's edge.

Standing in the middle of its tipping point, perfectly balanced.

On one side, my isolated life. On the other...

Fox.

And as he picks up the remote and asks, "What bad movie are we watching?"

I already know which way I've fallen.

Eleven

Fox

> FOX: Garbage person? (They make a lot of money)

DESSIE: 🌚 I don't do well with smells.

> FOX: I hate to break it to you, sugar, but hockey players smell after games.

DESSIE: Good thing there are showers at the rinks.

> FOX: *waggles brows GIF* Want to see them up close and personal?

DESSIE: The showers or the hockey players.

> FOX: 🐺 There's only ONE hockey player you're going to see up close and personal.

DESSIE: Does this mean that you've arrived at your new house?

FOX: I'm surrounded by far too many boxes.

DESSIE: Moving sucks.

FOX: And here I thought you were going to offer to help.

DESSIE: I have a very important job interview all of a sudden.

FOX: Where?

DESSIE: My bed.

FOX: Rude.

DESSIE: Fox?

FOX: Yeah?

DESSIE: I'll be down tomorrow to hang with Rosie and Bailey, do you want me to stop by?

FOX: Yes.

DESSIE: You sure?

FOX: Do I need to remind you about our conversation from last night?

DESSIE: No.

DESSIE: I'll be there around five.

———

DESSIE: Nice goal, princess.

FOX: Just because it bounced off my ass and into the net doesn't make it count any less. How'd you even watch the game, anyway? It's not televised.

DESSIE: The team was streaming it on social media. I didn't see the whole thing, but I saw enough.

FOX: Great. 😒

DESSIE: Hey. I think it should have counted for twice as much considering it hit off both cheeks. 😏

FOX: Funny.

FOX: Still, gonna let the stats guy know.

DESSIE: I expect payment for my services in the form of cookies.

FOX: Noted. Next time you come down.

DESSIE: Which is code for you having more boxes for me to unpack.

FOX: Maybe.

FOX: So, did Roger let you back into the bar?

DESSIE: Only to have a drink. 😕 Though, he did let me show him how to run the inventory system. Or attempt to anyway. I have the feeling it's going to require some serious work getting it back into shape before long.

FOX: Maybe that's your way back on the payroll?

DESSIE: Sabotage? I like the way you think.

DESSIE: But in reality, I'm just back on Boomer Tech support. But we cleared the air, and he agreed to let me help out as long as I promise to keep looking for—his words: a real job.

FOX: Progress then.

DESSIE: In everything except figuring out what I actually want to do with this next chapter of my life.

FOX: I've got more ideas.

DESSIE: More time to troll the internet for ideas that will make me crazy, you mean?

FOX: Now you're getting it, sugar. 😉 And so...speaking of your IT skills—did you ever think about putting those to use in other ways?

DESSIE: Um...is this some sort of weird proposition that's going to have me selling feet pics?

FOX: Well, now that you mention it...

DESSIE: Good night, Fox.

DESSIE: But no, I don't think IT is my future.

FOX: I'll keep looking.

FOX: Night, sugar.

———

FOX: Marine biologist.

DESSIE: I hate to continue to be the Negative
Nelly, but I get seasick.

FOX: *sigh* 😔

DESSIE: I'm hopeless.

FOX: We'll figure it out.

DESSIE: Right now I want to talk about
anything that isn't me and my empty future.

FOX: Are you coming down soon?

DESSIE: In a couple of days.

DESSIE: Did you talk to Rosie?

FOX: About Annie?

DESSIE: Yeah.

FOX: Yeah.

DESSIE: And?

FOX: And it's still weird, but it's Rosie. You
know she won't hold it against me. It's just...
another fucked up thing courtesy of the
Donovan clan.

FOX: Plus, she was already family. The only difference is that we know we share some genes.

DESSIE: How mature of you both.

FOX: Don't worry. I'm still looking for that frog to hide in your desk.

DESSIE: How was practice?

FOX: Pucks and sticks and my teammates trying to figure out why I'm smiling like an idiot all the time.

DESSIE: Well...

FOX: Well what?

DESSIE: Did they figure it out?

FOX: We're all spending a ton of time in close contact with little to keep us busy, what do you think, sugar?

DESSIE: That hockey players gossip worse than the citizens of River's Bend.

FOX: Bingo.

FOX: They know it's a woman and they want to meet you. Especially Smitty.

DESSIE: That's...terrifying.

FOX: Apparently he dreams of being a matchmaker.

DESSIE: Also terrifying.

FOX: I told him I'm already matched up.

DESSIE: ...

FOX: Too much?

DESSIE: I...

DESSIE: For once, I think that it might not be enough.

FOX: Fuck.

DESSIE: What?

FOX: I wish it was a five minute drive away so I could come over and kiss you for that.

DESSIE: Good.

FOX: It's good I'm getting blue balls from missing you?

DESSIE: It's good because it means you still want me to come down tomorrow.

FOX: I want you to come down forever.

DESSIE: ...

FOX: Too much?

DESSIE: Maybe.

DESSIE: But I think...I like it.

DESSIE: Good luck at the preseason game.

DESSIE: See you tomorrow.

———

DESSIE: Sorry the game went to hell.

FOX: It happens sometimes.

DESSIE: I'm still sorry. How's the eye?

FOX: Feels like I got into a fight.

DESSIE: Because you did?

FOX: There's that.

DESSIE: It looked like it hurt.

FOX: Lucky for me, I've got a hard head.

DESSIE: Still looks like it hurt.

FOX: I'm fine, sugar. But it's cute that you're worried.

DESSIE: I'm not worried.

DESSIE: You've got ice on it, though?

FOX: *sends pic of ice-covered face*

FOX: Now get some rest, sugar. I'll see you tomorrow when I get home?

DESSIE: What time does the plane land?

FOX: Three.

DESSIE: Then five or so? I promised Bailey that I'd hang out for a bit.

FOX: Anything you want, sugar lips.

DESSIE: That's a dangerous thing to say.

FOX: Doesn't make it any less true.

FOX: And I'm glad you've been hanging out with your friends.

DESSIE: We're brainstorming for jobs.

DESSIE: And, for the record, no one has
suggested anything to do with poles.

FOX: Amateurs.

DESSIE: 🥀 Good night. Safe travels.

FOX: Night, sugar.

———

I'm tempted to go by Bailey's on my way home from the rink.

But I'm tired, am overdue for a shower—no stinky hockey players for my girl—and then I need to make sure my place isn't a disaster for when Dessie comes over.

Yeah, plane rides are so much better than the buses we spent hours on when I was playing with the Rush, but even in the big leagues, we still have to get to and from the airport. So...more bus rides, just shorter ones.

Now I'm driving back to my house and resisting the urge to get my fill of Dessie. Texting isn't nearly enough, not now that I've given in to my need for her.

Not now that I'm determined to make her mine.

I need to touch her, to smell her, to feel the silk of her hair, her skin.

To taste her.

But...progress.

So, in an effort to continue with Plan Patience, I drive straight to my house.

I'm exhausted, my back aches from sitting on the plane, from the physical game the night before. And I have a fucking black eye.

Ugh.

Am I grumpy when I have no reason to be?

Yes.

But am I going to do anything about that?

Nope.

I'll be surly through a long hot shower, shoving some food in my mouth, and then waiting for her to show up.

Then I'll be in a better mood.

There. Plan. Go.

But it's not my plan for very long, I realize as I pull into my driveway, my heart skipping a beat when I see who's sitting on my front porch.

I shove the transmission into park, turn off the engine, and fly out of my driver's side door almost before I realize I've moved.

Not patient.

Very *not* patient.

Very *not* according to plan.

Thankfully, Dessie seems as impatient as me. She runs down the walkway, the bags in her hands swinging, her smile wide and beautiful enough to make my heart skip a beat.

At least until she all but skids to a stop in front of me, her expression sobering.

I close the rest of the distance between us, cup her jaw. "What's up, sugar?"

"Is this—?" She pauses, biting her lip.

"Is this what?"

Her eyes slip from mine. "Is this okay?" she asks softly. "Me surprising you like this?"

I inhale, stepping forward and cupping her face in my cheeks. "You're always welcome."

"Even though I didn't tell you I was coming?"

"This is the *best* surprise ever," I tell her, holding her gaze for long enough that she knows I mean it. "Now," I say, nudging her toward my open garage. "Did you finish with Bailey early? Or was that just to throw me off your scent?"

More nibbling. "There wasn't an order." A beat. "But there still wasn't a discussion about poles."

I smile because she's funny, but it's my heart that's in trouble. It pounds as I ask, "So you just wanted to see me?"

Pink on her cheeks, but her voice is steady. "Is that so hard to believe?"

"Nope." I step back and fist pump. "That Fox Brown charm is finally growing on you."

"Like a fungus," she quips.

I chuckle then take the bags from her hands, gripping them in one of mine, and all but herding her into the garage.

No escaping. Not now.

"What have you got in these, anyway?" I tease. "Bricks?"

A glance down shows her flush spreading. "Um, no," she whispers. "I just—"

When she doesn't go on, I open the door to the house and usher her into my mud room. "You just *what*, sugar lips?"

Her eyes meet mine for a heartbeat. "Well, I thought"—the pink turns to bright red—"I just...you've been helping me with my whole thing." She waves her hand.

I lift my brows in question.

"Helping me figure out my next steps," she explains. "And bringing me dinner and coffee and cookies and I just..."

I close the door, draw us down the hall while I wait for her to answer, setting the bags on the kitchen counter.

"Well, I just thought maybe I could cook for you, and we could..." She takes a deep breath and reaches into one of the totes. "Well, I thought I could return the favor by cooking you chicken parmesan before we watch this."

She pulls her hand out with a flourish...

And everything inside me freezes.

TWELVE

DESSIE

"How do you know about that?" he rasps and the nerves in my stomach ramp up.

There's a fucking tornado happening inside me, and I struggle to keep my expression placid, to not turn and haul ass out of his house.

This is...

Well, this is the biggest step I've taken since—

Jett.

"Fuck, sugar," he growls, and I jump, nearly bolt.

But before I can so much as skitter back a step, his big arms are wrapping around me and he's hauling me against his chest in a tight hug that squeezes every bit of fear out of my body.

"How'd you know?" he asks.

"About the food or the movie?" I manage to push out, my lungs protesting.

This is terrifying and yet...I know that I'm not leaving.

Maybe my picker is still broken, maybe I'll get hurt in the end, maybe this will all go wrong...

But I don't think so.

Fox is...

Well, I've never felt like this before.

And I've never had someone treat me like this before.

So...I've decided to pull on my big girl pants and see this through to the end.

"Either," he says, smoothing his big hand up and down my back. "Both."

I dare to reach up and hug him back, to press my front fully to his, to rise on tiptoe and settle my hands on his broad shoulders. "I pay attention too."

And then he does the most wonderful thing.

He smiles at me, drops his forehead against mine. "Fuck, sugar."

"What?"

"I knew I liked you," he whispers. "Right from the beginning, I knew it."

My pulse pounds through my veins.

"But I didn't know it would be this easy to love you."

I inhale, everything cell in my body freezing and then realigning. Unlocking. Opening up to...

Fox.

He bends his head, pressing his mouth to mine, and...

It's *everything*.

Soft but with the lightest brush of rough from his beard. Confident, his lips parting mine without preamble. *Hot*—his tongue sweeping in to tangle with mine. His groan vibrates through his chest and then he's lifting me up, setting me on the counter, stepping between my thighs, and kissing me until my lungs protest, until my heart's pounding, until I'm basically a melted pile of goo.

"Goddamn, sugar," he rasps when he pulls his mouth from mine.

"It's your fault," I say.

"Yours," he counters, cupping my jaw. "For giving me this."

"It's just a movie and dinner."

"No." He presses his lips to mine for a brief but intense kiss. "You're giving me *you*."

He's not wrong.

Even if I can't give voice to that fact yet.

He taps his finger to the tip of my nose. "And I knew you'd taste sweet as sugar." A wink as he lifts me down then lightly swats my ass. "Now am I parking my ass on a stool and watching you cook my favorite meal? Or are you putting me to work?"

———

The man can chop some veggies.

And he didn't get mad when I got distracted watching him and burned the sauce, making him have to run out and get replacement ingredients.

And his face when he saw what I brought for dessert?

I'll never forget it.

Or the kiss he laid on me afterward.

It's just chocolate pie from River's Bend's bakery and home-made whipped cream.

But we both know it's more. *So* much more.

Now, we're both full of chicken and pasta and pie, and I'm sitting on the couch as he loads up the movie. Thank God he has a video game console to play it on, though I guess we could have streamed it from somewhere.

It wouldn't have been the same, though.

Yeah, it's silly, but I like this better.

There's something about falling into the ritual of opening up a DVD case, pulling out the disc and putting it into the player, then sitting back as the movie's home screen fills the TV screen that feels right.

"You know," he says, pointing the remote at the screen and changing the input so that we see that home screen, "I know that I've been striking out on the whole job search thing, but maybe I've been focusing on the wrong thing."

I tilt my head to the side, study him closely. "What do you mean?"

He sits down next me. "Have you ever thought about going back to school?"

My first instinct is to say no freaking way, but...

There's something that stops me.

He tracks that hesitation.

"Well, that's not an immediate no," he says lightly.

"No, it's not." I let him tuck me into his side. "I just..."

"What would you want to study?"

"It's silly," I say, "but I always thought it would be interesting to take business classes."

"Yes." He snaps his fingers. "That's perfect! Business management."

"What?"

"The inventory at the bar. The new ordering system. Streamlining the kitchen. You've got Monroe's working more efficiently than ever. And that wouldn't just be a one-off. You'd be great at it."

"I—"

He turns to me, huge smile on his face, and it calls to that kernel of excitement inside me.

"You know what? I think I could be."

"I *know* you would be," he says, touching my cheek, "but no hard sell on my front. Think about it? Sit in it? And then if it feels right we'll figure out the next steps?"

If it feels right *we'll*—

I love him.

I love this man, and I probably have for far longer than I'm willing to admit.

But before I can find the courage to give voice to that thought, the movie starts to play.

And then I'm sitting next to man I love, watching his favorite movie.

Pretty Woman.

———

The last thing I remember is the gorgeous Julia Roberts covered in bubbles.

The next thing I'm aware of is...

Movement.

My eyes fly open, and I realize that Fox has me cradled against his chest and is carrying me upstairs.

"Shh, sugar," he murmurs, holding me a little tighter. "I'll tuck you in bed then go sleep downstairs. Don't worry."

"I can make it home," I say.

"I know you can." He bends and settles me on something soft —a bed, I deduce with my excellent reasoning skills. "But it's a long drive and I'll worry. So, you're going to stay and sleep here."

"Is that an order?"

He flicks on the bedside lamp, illuminating the room with softly glowing light. He's smiling but there's a thread of steel in his eyes, and I know he'll fight me on this...because he cares. "Do I need to make it one?" he asks quietly.

"Do you like playing dangerous games?" I counter.

Now his smile turns wicked. "Only with you."

My pussy spasms. "*Fox.*"

A hand on my cheek. "Sleep, sugar lips," he says—or rather orders (and settles warmly against my heart, same as the previous one). "I'll see you in the morning." He tugs the blankets up and over me. "Night."

I catch his hand before he can leave. "Or you could stay," I say softly. "Stay and sleep with me."

Heat in his eyes. "I wouldn't be able to just sleep, sugar."

Another spasm, heat and desire gathering between my legs. "That's okay," I tell him. "I wouldn't be able to *just sleep* either."

For a moment, he doesn't move.

Then his fingers tighten around mine, our gazes connect, and the need in his deep brown eyes steals the last of the air from my lungs. "You sure?" he asks gruffly.

In answer, I use my free hand to find the corner of the blanket he tucked over me and toss it back.

"Kind of need the words, sugar," he says, his fingers flexing around mine, his body tense and poised on razor's edge.

I don't even have a moment of hesitation before I tell him, "I'm sure."

For a heartbeat, he doesn't move—but then...he *does*.

His body comes over mine, pressing me into the mattress. He's heavy—not unpleasantly so, especially when he braces himself on his elbows, one on either side of my head, and his legs settle between mine.

"*Oh*," I whisper when I find my pelvis suddenly cradling his.

So that I feel *all* of him.

It's glorious.

And big.

And *mine*.

"Like that, sugar?" he asks with a wicked smile.

"Yes"—I hook a leg around his hip—"though I'm hoping it's going to get better."

"Oh, it's going to *get better*." He shifts so that one of his hands is free and trails it up along my side. At the same time, he drops his head, pressing our mouths together, and the kiss he gives me makes me forget to breathe, makes me forget to think, makes me forget to do anything except to *want*.

"God, sugar," he rumbles as his fingers find the hem of my T-shirt and slip beneath the fabric to caress my side. "Your skin is like silk."

His fingertips are rough, the calluses from hockey abrading my skin in the best way. I shiver, goose bumps rising on my flesh, but he doesn't stop, just continues shoving the fabric of my shirt up, exposing more and more of my flesh to that heated gaze of his.

When it's bunched up just beneath my breasts, he shifts again, giving it one quick tug and pulling it over my head.

The fabric flies across the room and then he's reaching beneath me, undoing the clasp of my bra, tugging the straps down my shoulders, my arms, tossing that scrap of material to the side just as quickly as he'd done my shirt.

"Fuck," he growls, "you're beautiful."

And I've never felt more so.

It's impossible to do anything but believe those words with the desire etched into his expression, the need blazing through his eyes, the gentle, reverent way he touches me.

One big palm cups my breast, kneading my flesh.

"Oh, God," I moan when his thumb traces over the hardened bud of my nipple. He rolls it between thumb and forefinger, putting those roughened fingertips to good use and I can't hold still. I grind against him, riding the hard ridge of his erection, feeling my pleasure build to almost desperate levels.

I'm ready to explode.

Need for this man, need for *more*—it tears through me.

I have to get naked, have to touch him, have to feel him inside me.

Luckily, he seems to read that desperation in me and drops his head, kissing his way along my jaw, down my throat, pausing at my breasts.

"These tits are fucking *mine*."

He sucks at my nipple, sending wave after wave of pleasure through me and my fingers dive into his hair, holding his mouth against me, keeping him there, soaking in the sensation—the heat of his mouth, the rough stroke of his beard on my skin, the flash of his teeth, the soothing stroke of his tongue.

I gasp as he switches sides.

Rubbing that beard along the underside of my breast, pinching my nipple hard enough to make me gasp then assuaging the sting with his tongue. It's teeth and lips, touch and teasing, but not *hurry*.

Because he even though desire is ripping through me, *he's* not in any rush. He takes his time worshiping my breasts slowly before kissing his way down my abdomen, inch by inch.

A flick opens the button of my jeans.

A nudge pushes them down, down, *off*.

And then his fingertips are playing with the waistband of my underwear, drawing it down an inch, kissing the exposed flesh before coaxing it down another inch. Then another, another, *another*. Until I'm completely exposed to him.

He parts my legs, tossing one over each shoulder, and—

His tongue traces through my folds, a sleek, hot brand that arrows in on where I need him the most.

"Fuck," he rasps, eyes blazing into mine. "Sweet, so fucking sweet."

And then he goes back to ravaging my pussy with his mouth, putting his beard to good use, dragging it over my sensitive flesh. His tongue circles my clit and he nibbles, lightly teasing that sensitive bud with his teeth, ratcheting my pleasure even higher.

Every muscle in my body is taut.

Every cell is on knife's edge.

My lungs are heaving. My eyes are unfocused, my thighs are squeezing so tightly around his neck and shoulders that he might not be able to breathe, but I can't bring myself to loosen my hold, can't do anything but stay poised on that narrow edge when he slides a finger inside me.

It's thick and hard, and he curls it up, stroking against the inner walls of my pussy.

I shudder, that pleasure closing in.

"Fox," I plead, not wanting to go without him.

"No, sugar." He slips another finger in and orders, "*Come*," thrusting hard and deep inside of me...

And I have no choice.

There's no stopping it.

The train is barreling down the tracks, the countdown has begun to send the rocket off into space, the boulder is rolling down the hill threatening everything at the bottom...

And my orgasm is tearing through me.

THIRTEEN

FOX

Her tight little cunt is squeezing my fingers like a vise and that's fucking beautiful.

Just not as remotely beautiful as her face is when she comes apart.

The flush on her cheeks spreads down her throat, across her chest, making me desperate to taste those tits again, to have the hardened peaks of her nipples on my tongue. I want to have her moans on my tongue, want to feel her grinding not just against my palm, her pussy clamping around my fingers, but I want her beneath me, want her pulsing around my dick as she cries out.

But...patience.

We skipped a lot of steps tonight, kissing to getting my mouth on her—and though my brain is spinning with the urge to crawl between her thighs and fuck her hard and fast, I know we should wait.

Only...

I don't anticipate her next move.

Hell, who am I kidding?

I can *never* anticipate her next move.

One second, she's lax as I'm lapping up the evidence of her desire, the taste of that sweet pussy on my tongue as I war with myself, never wanting to move, but also desperate to fuck her.

And the next, I find myself flat on my back.

Dessie clambers on top of me, the slick heat of her cunt brushing my stomach, the head of my cock, and then she's lowering herself onto me.

"Fuck," I groan as the tight sheath of her comes down over me in one smooth movement.

"Yes, *God*," she moans her palms settling on the middle of my chest, her ass hitting the tops of my thighs as she seats herself fully onto me.

"Condom," I grit out, reaching for her thighs, intending to tug her off me.

"Fuck." She goes still, her eyes going wide. "I'm sorry. I—"

"No, sugar," I say. "It's okay. I'm clean. I just...this is a big step."

Her throat works and my eyes nearly roll into the back of my head when she pulses around me. "I'm on the pill," she says, "and I know it's stupid, but I don't want to stop." Her hips shift ever so slightly, rocking against me, her gaze connecting with mine. "I'm clean too. I—" A breath. "I was tested after—" She shakes her head.

"Sugar," I murmur, cupping the side of her throat. "It's okay."

I know it's stupid. But I don't want to her to stop either.

I've never gone bare with any other woman, never taken this risk, never allowed myself to be this vulnerable, but with Dessie... it just seems right.

This is the woman I love, the woman I want to spend the rest of my life with.

And it doesn't feel like a risk, not really.

If she's safe, if she feels comfortable, if she wants it—

Fuck, I would give her anything.

And it's not like I'm sacrificing myself here.

The slick heat of her pussy clamping around my dick is the best thing I've ever felt in my life.

Better than being drafted, better than winning the Calder cup, better than knowing that I have enough money in the bank that I'll never have to want for anything. Better even than that first step onto the ice in the Grizzlies' home arena, the crowd screaming, my dreams being fulfilled.

But...not better than her smiles, the shy way she looked at me today, those bags of groceries between us.

Not better than this feeling right now.

Being this close to her.

"I'll get a condom," she says, starting to lift off me.

I clamp my hands onto her hips.

"No," I order roughly. "I don't want you to move, sugar."

"No?" she asks, and I see the first hint of the mischief that I love so much about her, the confidence that had been dimmed except for very special occasions until recently.

Until *me*.

Until *I* helped her find her way out.

Yeah, I might as well be a fucking superhero.

"You *don't* want me to move?"

Her voice is teasing and paired with her internal muscles squeezing, her fingernails biting lightly into my chest...

Well, maybe she's the one with the superpowers.

She rocks forward, squeezing me tight—

I bite back a curse, know she's doing it on purpose to drive me crazy.

And it's working.

She bends toward me, her lips almost coming to mine, her words glazing along my bottom lip. "You don't want me to move?" she asks again.

I grit my teeth as sweat begins to bead on my forehead, as it gathers and drips down between my shoulder blades. The urge to roll us, to plunge deep into that tight, slick cunt, to fuck her hard and fast and furiously until we're both there, is nearly over-whelming.

But this is Dessie—smiling, bright, beautiful, Dessie.

And I won't take this moment away from her.

Not fucking *ever*.

So, I clench the blankets in my fists, and I grab tight to my control, and I hold myself still as I say, "I want you to move however it makes you feel good, sugar."

"And if I say I think I'd like to stay *right* here?" she drawls, dragging one of her fingernails along my chest.

I flex my hips, shifting my cock inside her, hitting that spot I'd found a few minutes earlier with my fingers, making her gasp and rock against me, taking me deeper. "I think I can change your mind."

"Not fair," she huffs.

"You like it," I counter.

I know she does.

Because she's moving faster, lifting up and sliding down on me, eroding my control effortlessly.

"Mmm." A beat as she lifts. Then descends. "Maybe."

I grin, bend at the waist to kiss her.

"Air," she gasps, pushing at my chest long moments later.

"Overrated," I pant out, my lungs sawing.

But, thankfully, she finally decides to put us both out of our misery, and she starts fucking me in earnest, lifting up on my cock and grinding down, dragging that sweet cunt against my pelvis, taking me deep inside her, those inner muscles clenching me tightly enough that I see stars.

My control snaps and I thrust up into her.

"Yes," she moans. "Like that."

So, I do it again and again and *again*, until we're both pant-ing, until our sweat-covered bodies are coming together in a rhythm that's frenzied and out of control and fucking perfect.

Until I sense that she's right there, and I know I can finally let go.

"Fuck!" I shout, my hips pistoning up into her, meeting her movements each time she grinds down.

Once. Twice—

She cries out, her orgasm rippling around my cock, milking me as I come inside her so hard that, swear to fuck, I black out.

It's a Herculean effort that I somehow manage to rouse myself long minutes—maybe a fucking century—later in order to carry her into the bathroom, to let her do her business. When that's done, I hand her a damp cloth, help her clean up. Then I tug one of my T shirts over her head, brush her hair out of her face, and carry her back into the bedroom.

My legs are shaking and I'm exhausted, as though I played a double header, but I get us over to the bed, settle her on the mattress and drop down beside her. Groaning, I toss the blankets over us, gather her closer, and let sleep come, knowing that the next morning is going to be the best ever.

I just...

Couldn't have known right then how wrong I was going to be.

Fourteen

Dessie

S o, sneaking out after groundbreaking sex definitely wasn't the right move.

I know that—well, I suppose I knew it from the moment I'd slipped out of Fox's warm arms, but...

I hadn't been thinking then.

Because, the next thing I knew, I was driving out of town.

Okay, not just *out of town* but two and a half hours up to River's Bend.

In silence—just raw-dogging the fuck out of the hours' long drive until I pull to a stop in front of Bailey and Axel's ranch house.

It's only then that I snap out of it.

And realize what I've done.

And know what I have to fix.

Immediately, I snatch my phone, see that I have a half-dozen calls and even more texts from Fox.

Quickly, I hit his number, try to call him.

But it just rings and rings and *rings*.

"Dammit," I mutter, looking at the clock, realizing that he's probably at practice. I start to type out a text, stop.

How the hell can I explain why I left?

> DESSIE: I panicked this morning and—

I stop. Delete that because it feels very much like...

An excuse.

> DESSIE: Fox. I messed up. I shouldn't have—

Left. Well obviously.

"Come on, Madden," I whisper, trying to psyche myself up. Or get my brain to work enough to not say something dumb as hell.

> DESSIE: I'm sorry.

"Ugh," I whisper, but I still hit send.

It's not enough. Not nearly. But I know I need to start there.

And then I need to get my ass back to San Jose and make this right in person.

Unfortunately, before I can turn my car around and get the hell out of here, there's a knock on my window...

And I see my friends peering at me through the glass.

"Damn," I whisper.

———

"These are really good," I say, shoving the apple turnover in my mouth and chugging my coffee like it's water. "That's why I came over. I had a hankering for baked goods."

I shove more of the pastry in my mouth as my friends exchange a look telling me they don't by my bullshit in the least.

"Hankering?" Rosie mouths to Bailey.

"Hmm," is Bailey's only response.

"I'm fine, guys," I say. "Really." I drain the dredges of my coffee, know that I should get the hell out of here.

Back on the road. Back to San Jose.

"Liar, liar pants on fire," Rosie says, her curls bouncing.

"What are you even doing in town, anyway?" I mutter. "I thought you were both in San Francisco."

Bailey studies me closely. "I had to check on some things with the cattle—which you know because we talked yesterday."

"Right," I lie, because I had, in fact, *not* remembered. I set my mug down. "Did everything go okay with that?"

Her face gentles. "Yes," she says. "But Des—"

I stand up. "I should go."

"We love you, you know that right, Dessie girl?" Rosie says, snagging my hand and holding me in place when I try to make a break for it. "But, honey, now that I'm not trying to rebuild a town and wade through a legal mess, I suddenly have a lot more time on my hands." Her expression becomes shrewd. "Which is why I know you've been busy."

My cheeks heat. "It's not that big of a deal."

Rosie rolls her eyes and glances at Bailey. "What do we think of that?"

"More lying," Bailey says dryly. "And it's like she's not even putting any real effort into it."

I scowl. "You guys—"

"We've given you a lot of rope," Rosie says, as though I didn't speak. "And I don't mean what's happening with Fox. That's... well, that's a story for another day and although I want the details at some point—"

Details of how much I fucked up?

Yeah, *those* I can provide.

"—that's not the most important thing right now."

"It's enough, Des." Bailey leans forward, takes my other hand, dragging me away from Rosie and back over to the couch, drawing me down to sit next to her. "You need to spill it and let us help you through whatever's hurting you like you've helped us through our bullshit. We're your best friends and—"

"I'm in love with Fox."

The total blurt has them both freezing, but Billie Rose recovers first. "Excuse me?"

"I—I—" Goddamn it. "I know you said you could wait on the details, but the truth is that I've told Fox everything," I whisper. "About my exes and about my ex-fiancé—" I squeeze Bailey's hand, glance over at Rosie, my tone an apology. "I haven't been good about sharing with you and you both deserve better. I just... I was ashamed that I kept choosing so poorly, ashamed that I dated a man who fucked with my job, and even more ashamed when I realized that I hadn't wanted the job in the first place."

"Why would you be ashamed that some asshole hurt you?" Bailey asks softly. "Or that you didn't want to keep working at the station?"

I want to lock down these feelings, want to pretend I'm fine and the shame isn't there, but it is.

And...I need to be done hiding.

"I was supposed to leave River's Bend and kick ass. Supposed to be fearless and break barriers and save lives."

Rosie's fingers tighten around mine. "But you did all of that."

My chest loosens. "Yeah," I say. "I guess I did. I just..."

"Didn't love it," she murmurs.'

"No," I agree. "I think I held on so tight to this idea for so long, it seemed like a failure to admit it wasn't for me."

Bailey's mouth kicks up. "I feel that."

"Word," Rosie adds, coming over to sit next to me.

"Really?" I ask.

They both nod.

"I felt pathetic that I was relieved that Jett cheated on me—it gave me an excuse to leave," I add when their brows drag together.

"But not *only* that," Rosie says.

I still.

"Or am I wrong?"

I wrinkle my nose and glance at Bailey. "Why is she always right?"

"It's a skill," she says, buffing her knuckles on her shoulder.

"An annoying one," Bailey mutters. "But she's right. What else, Des?"

"It allowed me to keep hiding. If something was wrong with me, if I couldn't choose right, if all men hurt me..." I trail off, hearing myself and realizing how much of a coward I was. "Ugh," I mutter, scrubbing my hands over my face.

"Reality strikes?" Bailey teases.

I drop my hands and scowl at them. "It was easier to pretend to believe all of that than to acknowledge that I wanted...well, that I wanted what you both have." A sigh. "Because if I *did* admit it then I'd have to actually do something about it."

"And this is where Fox comes in?" Bailey asks.

My cheeks heat.

"I thought you couldn't stand him," she says softly.

"Oh, young matchmaker in training," Rosie interjects, nudging Bailey's foot with her own, "have you learned nothing?"

Bailey sighs and leans back against the cushions. "Just because you and Joel started off on the wrong foot—"

"Handcuffs?" Rosie reminds her. "A naked, grumpy hockey playboy trapped on your porch?"

Bailey narrows her eyes. "You're hilarious."

"Turns out," I tell them, interrupting what will surely devolve into an argument about them intervening in each other's lives (something, for the record, both of them have gotten really good at—starting with Rosie playing matchmaker with Bailey and Axel and those handcuffs, and ending with Bailey dishing it right back out when Rosie got with Joel). "It turns out that I liked Fox a little too much. But..." A breath for courage before I fill them in about him showing up on my doorstep and the cookies and coffee and him comforting me when my uncle fired me and helping me figure out my next steps career-wise, and...

Well, I tell them *all* of it.

"And I guess," I say as they stare at me with wide eyes. "I finally realized that even if most of my life is in limbo, there's one thing I want for certain...and that's Fox."

Bailey smiles.

Rosie bumps her shoulder against mine. "Proud of you, kid."

"Well, you'll be proud until you find out what I did next."

Sober expressions great me before Bailey says, "Whatever you did, we'll still love you."

My heart squeezes. "Don't make me cry."

"Meh," Rosie teases. "Cry away. I always have tissues in my purse."

Bailey swats her. "Stop." Her eyes narrow in my direction. "But seriously. Now you need to spill the rest of it."

So, I do.

I tell them how I panicked and know I fucked up and that I need to find a way to make it right and...

I do cry.

But at the end of that, they still love me.

And then they help me plan how to make it right with Fox...

Before I haul my butt back to San Jose.

FIFTEEN

Fox

I wind up and put every bit of my strength into the shot, sending it tearing through the air and into the back of the net with a satisfying *thunk*.

And then I grab another puck from the bucket I'd dumped out at my feet and go again.

And again.

Shot after shot until my arms ache and sweat is dripping between my shoulder blades and I turn to see Joel leaning against the boards, watching me with shrewd eyes.

Fuck.

Sighing, I shove my stick into the empty bucket, skate with it over to the net then drop to my knees and start picking them up.

He follows—because of course he fucking does.

"You shouldn't even be at this rink," I mutter when all he does is lean on the net and stare at me.

"Lucky for you, I'm only a short drive away," he says then adds, when I don't reply, "Okay, what gives?"

"With what?"

"The puck murder."

Fucker's funny, but I don't feel like laughing.

She was gone.

Just gone.

We'd shared all that and—

Gone.

Just fucking gone when I woke up, her side of the bed empty and cold, her car no longer parked at the curb in front of my house. And not answering her phone.

I'd told her I loved her and...

Fucking *gone.*

Now, am I going to let her get away with that shit? No fucking way. But am I pissed as hell and going to lick my wounds for a few hours before I track her down?

Yes.

So, grinding my teeth together, I don't bite at Joel's fishing expedition. I just keep picking up pucks and dropping them into the bucket. And then don't stop until all of them are picked up.

Unfortunately, Joel isn't as easy to get rid of.

He just stays there, reclining against the goal.

"I'm just getting some ice time in," I mutter.

He snorts, pushes off the goal and starts trailing me when I shove my stick into the bucket again and skate over to the bench with it. I heft it up onto the bench and start walking down the hall.

And Joel's right there.

"You know," he says, "you were awfully cheerful these last couple weeks." A long, pointed pause. "And you're awfully pissed today."

Jesus Christ.

Clenching my teeth together so tightly that a bolt of pain shoots through my jaw, I resist the urge to plow my fist into his face. First, he's too pretty for that. Second, I'm in a shit mood and it's not his fault.

Third...

Well, I don't really have a third, except to say that he's my friend and a good guy and...I don't go around punching my friends.

Even when they're being fucking annoying.

"Your point?" I grind out.

"My *point* is that you've gone from whistling that annoying little tune of yours," he says, "to..."

"Murdering pucks?" I ask quietly.

"Exactly." His lips twitch. "Which speaks of only one thing."

I pause just outside the locker room and glance over at him, lifting an eyebrow in question.

"Woman trouble."

My jaw tenses further and I know the asshole clocks it because he smirks. "Dessie?"

"Dude," I mutter.

"I fucking knew it."

"I didn't say it was her."

"I still heard you say her name." He leans closer. "Plus, Rosie clued me in."

That's not helpful.

"How's it going with the Gold?" I ask, trying to distract him.

His eyes dance, and I immediately know he sees right through me, but before I can pivot, he just says, "Great." Then he shrugs. "So, how'd you fuck up with Dessie?"

I exhale and scrub my hands over my face. "I finally got in there, man. Behind the barbed wire and past the steel-lined walls. I thought we were going to be smooth-sailing for once and..."

"What?"

"I woke up after the best orgasm of my life"—he smirks—"after all but telling her that I love her and"—his eyes widen—"she was gone."

"Too much too fast?"

I groan and shove my hair out of my face. "I didn't think so, considering that she stayed and cooked me dinner after I told her how I feel, that she made the first fucking move to"—our eyes connect—"you know."

He nods.

"She was..." I sigh and push through the locker room door, thankful it's empty and my new teammates are nowhere in sight. "I thought she was finally all in."

"Have you talked to her?"

I exhale. "No," I mutter, dropping onto the bench. "I must have called at least a dozen times, and she didn't return any of my texts, see?" I pull out my phone, start to show him the blank screen.

Only it's not blank.

There's a call.

And a text.

My heart squeezes hard as I read.

> DESSIE: I'm sorry.

"She called?" he asks, leaning over my shoulder.

I nod. "And texted," I say, lifting my phone to show him the screen.

He curses softly then looks back at me. "Want me to call Rosie and turn her loose on it?"

"Nah," I mutter. "You guys have just made it through the shit. I'll clean up my own house."

He exhales and I can see that he's warring with himself, but in the end, he just claps me on the shoulder and says, "It's worth it, you know. The struggle. The worry. The work to get there."

I nod goodbye to him as he walks out then haul my ass into the showers.

I don't go home.

Instead, I drive up to River's Bend, head directly to Dessie's apartment, and even though the parking lot behind Monroe's is devoid of her sedan, I still climb the stairs to her front door, still knock and listen for any sounds inside.

It's silent.

Not a hint of a bad movie in earshot.

"Fuck," I mutter, glancing down at my phone, hoping that it will magically ring again.

When it doesn't, I call her.

Ring. Ring. Ring. And then voicemail.

And no reply to another half-dozen texts.

My temple throbbing, I groan and get back in my car.

And then I drive all the way back home to San Jose, intending to get drunk and forget all about this shit for tonight.

I'll regroup in the morning, make another plan—call Rosie and Bailey into service if necessary.

But tonight I'm going to be miserable.

And drunk.

And—

Only when I pull up to my house...my porch isn't empty.

Sixteen

DESSIE

He's been gone a long time—much longer than his practice should have taken.

And even though I spilled my guts to my friends—and feel about a hundred pounds lighter because of it—even though I have a plan—which doesn't necessarily make me feel better, but at least I have a freaking plan, I'm not sure I can fix this.

"Breathe," I whisper, cursing that my phone died a couple of hours ago.

That I was so out of it, I didn't think to grab a charger from home and—

"Stop," I say. "It's going to be okay."

I'll apologize.

Explain.

And hopefully not have alienated him so much that he's changed his mind about moving forward.

And...

I need to tell him that I love him.

Which hopefully won't send *him* running for the fucking hills like a dumbass who doesn't know a good thing when she finally finds it—or rather when it finds *her*.

None of which gets him here any sooner.

None of which eases my ever-increasing nerves.

None of which—

The sound of an engine reaches my ears, and I whip my gaze down the street, straining to catch a glimpse of the car coming this way. My heart leaps when I see that it's Fox's and immediately my nerves amp up so high that I'm jittery, my hands shaking, my legs feeling like they won't hold me up.

But...

I have a plan.

And I'm going to execute it.

Apologize. Explain. I love you.

Apologize. Explain. I love you.

The car slows for a moment before returning to its previous speed and before I can even go down the three steps, he's whipped his car into the driveway and thrown open the driver's side door.

Apologize. Explain—

"I love you!" I shout the moment he's out of the car.

Not the plan. *So* not the plan.

Apologize first. Explain second. *Then* the *I love you* part.

But, even as anxious as I am, I still feel a blip of amusement when the big, bearded hockey player skids to a halt, his mouth dropping open. It's fleeting, though, and then he's rushing toward me again.

In the blink of an eye, he's in front of me. "What did you say?"

"I'm sorry," I tell him, gripping his forearms, holding his stare. "*So* sorry. Last night was perfect and I...I panicked. I was feeling so much, and you were so great, and this is...better than anything I've ever hoped for and I want more and—"

"Sugar." He slips from my hold to cup both sides of my face. "What did you say?"

Apologize. Check.

Explain. Sort of check.

Now—

"I love you."

He inhales sharply, that big chest expanding, and then...

He's moving again, wrapping his arms around me, dragging me against him. "Fuck, Dessie."

"I'm so sorry," I whisper. "I had a moment of insanity. It won't happen again."

"You scared the shit out of me," he rasps. "Especially when you wouldn't answer my calls." He pulls back, fixes me in place with a glare. "Promise me you won't do that again. Promise me that you'll talk to me, and if you can't, you'll at least text me and let me know you need some breathing room or leave a note or send fucking telegram or something."

"A telegram?" I giggle.

His face goes soft, and he settles his forehead against mine. "I wasn't going to let you go," he whispers. "But I'm fucking glad I don't have to chase you down."

He sounds tired. Exhausted.

"I'm so sorry," I say. "And I wasn't trying to avoid your calls the whole time. I..." I sigh and pull my phone from my pocket, showing him the darkened screen. "I forgot to bring a charger."

He tugs at a strand of my hair, rests his forehead against mine. "I'm just glad you're here now."

He stops and I frown. "What?"

An exhale. "You scared me."

More guilt. "I'm sor—"

"No more apologies." He presses his lips to mine. "We're celebrating tonight."

"I—"

I got the apology part, covered the I love you, but I haven't explained—

And I don't get to.

Because he scoops me up and carries me into the house.

And then he makes sure I'm so limp with pleasure that I can't even begin to think of leaving.

The best part?

I don't want to.

Epilogue

Dessie

"And then," I say, pointing at the computer screen that has my uncle squinting at the simple spreadsheet like it's the most complicated software code on the planet, "if you fill in this cell here—"

His bushy eyebrows drag together. "What's a cell again?"

"The little box here. See how my cursor— No, scratch that," I say, editing myself as I see the confusion creep into his eyes again. "See how the box has a darker outline around it?"

His scowl deepens but he leans in, squinting. Then he nods, says gruffly, "Yeah."

"So, you click there, put the numbers in, and hit this button..." I show him the ENTER button on the keyboard. "And that's it, the program will do the rest of it for you. Wanna try?"

I'm up in River's Bend, playing tech support again.

Read—I'm fixing the inventory spreadsheet and teaching my uncle how to not fuck it up again.

I shift back to give him a chance, supervise as he pecks at the keyboard, hits the ENTER key and we both watch as the inventory log updates.

"And," I add, leaning in and helping him move the mouse, "if you click here"—I navigate the cursor, my hand over his, to the next tab which I've set up so that he knows exactly what he needs to order. "Once you have your numbers, you can call your vendor, or *even*," I say with a flourish, waving my arm out to the side, "email it to them. Then they'll invoice you, you pay that, and *wham bam, thank you, ma'am,* you've got your supplies."

He's silent for a long moment, still scowling at the computer screen as though waiting for the other shoe to fall.

When it doesn't, his expression clears and he turns the chair, standing, and facing me. He squeezes me on the shoulder, his face softening. "When did you get so smart, Dessie girl?"

I grin, pat his hand, and joke, "Probably about the time you fired me."

There's guilt in my uncle's eyes, and even though I feel like a jerk for bringing it up like this, I also know this conversation is long overdue. It's been a month since I shouted at Fox across the driveway, blurting out my feelings for him.

A month where things have been quiet and easy. And not filled with insecurity or the past.

It's crazy because in these last weeks, I've had more *real*, more quiet moments and stolen kisses and feeling his fingertips trace nonsensical patterns on my skin than I've ever had in my life.

Because, somehow, that's become Fox and me.

Just us. Together. Learning to trust. Learning each other.

Fucking like rabbits every chance we get.

My lips curve. The orgasms are glorious, but Fox is...

Well, all I can say is that he's been more than I've ever hoped for.

It's small things—hanging at his house, alternating between romcoms and bad movies and cooking our favorite meals together. Then there are the sweet texts he sends checking on me when he's on the road and getting his opinion on which classes I should take at the local community college when the next semester starts.

It's all natural.

Perfect.

Us.

It's like now that I've stopped fighting it...

Everything has come together.

"Sweetheart," Uncle Roger begins, apology in his eyes.

"Hey," I say, "you did the right thing, you know you did."

His eyes cut away from mine, then come back. "Knowing doesn't make it any easier, kiddo."

"I'm going back to school," I tell him. "I wouldn't have even considered that if you let me keep hiding here."

"That's good, sweetheart," he says then sighs. "When you came back..."

"I was different," I say into the silence. "I..." I shake my head. "That happened for a lot of reasons, the least of which was that I was growing increasingly unhappy at work. Coming home was an excuse to avoid dealing with that and with all the other shit that was eating at me."

"Like what?" he asks, eyes narrowing.

"A relationship not working out," I tell him because I owe him that much. "And friends who weren't really my friends. I needed to come back to River's Bend for a reset, needed to be close to Rosie and Bailey again...the problem is that I got set back so far I don't think I would have ever moved forward without your help. And...without Fox's."

His mouth curves. "Knew it."

I roll my eyes. "What are you talking about?"

"I knew you and Fox would make it."

"But we fought constantly," I protest.

"Oil and water sometimes make the best combination."

"Isn't that literally the opposite of that idiom?"

"Idioms are stupid." He drops an arm around my shoulders and starts leading me from the office. "But my niece sure isn't."

My heart squeezes. My parents may not have been the most

engaged—they're good people, just...wrapped up in their own lives. But Uncle Roger has always been there.

"So in along vein..." I say.

He looks up at me, eyebrows raised.

"Think you can manage the inventory on your own?"

His mouth twitches. "I'll pay for the inevitable tech support."

"You'll be fine." I nudge his shoulder with mine then let him pull me into a quick hug.

"I know I will be," he says as I grab my purse and jacket.

"And I'm a phone call away if you need me."

"Don't you mean you're just upstairs?"

I still, smile. "No."

His brows shoot up, and my smile widens.

"Well, about Fox..."

"Yes?"

"Turns out that the college in San Jose is pretty good."

Those eyebrows shoot higher.

"And so Fox asked me to move in with him." My cheeks hurt from smiling so widely. "You know, to make the commute shorter."

"Right," he says, his tone dry.

"I'm ready to go out there and live."

My uncle nods approvingly. "I'll make sure to save plenty of glasses for you to polish when you deign to make it back to town, kid."

Grinning, I shake my head at him, then lean over the bar and kiss his cheek. "As long as you don't mess with my inventory system, I'll polish all the glasses you want."

We exchange goodbyes, which is really just me saying the words and him waving a hand in my direction before he disappears back into the stock room, and then I head outside to my car, thinking about the offer Fox had extended last night.

You're spending most of your time here as it is, sugar. Why don't you just make it official?

And...

My TV's better to watch all those crappy movies, right?

But other than that he hadn't pushed. Just made the offer, told me to think about it.

And...I had.

And—

I skid to a halt in the parking lot, eyes going wide at the sight of a big, burly hockey player carrying a box I'd packed this morning to my car.

My heart squeezes.

I'd thought about it.

And...I'm going to go for it.

Something Fox clearly knows.

He sets the box down and crosses over to me, his eyes dancing at what must be a shocked expression on my face.

"You knew what my answer was going to be?"

His beard twitches as he smiles. "Yeah, sugar lips, I knew." One broad shoulder lifts then drops. "It was my TV that put it over the edge for you, wasn't it?"

"Damn straight it was." I giggle then step into his arms, press my front to his. "I love you."

Gentle eyes. A tight embrace. A soft hand cupping my jaw. "You're my heart," he says simply in return.

My own heart rolls over in my chest, exposed and vulnerable and...

Completely safe.

It's why I can lift on tiptoe, press my lips to his, and know that the future may occasionally be messy and decidedly not bump-free, that he's likely always going to push my buttons, and that we will definitely fight over stupid things, but what we have together is...

Real.

It's not that my picker was broken...

I just needed a certain stubborn hockey player to realign it.

He pulls back, steals my keys, and begins loading the boxes into my car.

"Fox?"

"Yeah, sugar?"

"It was the TV."

His mouth twitches.

"But it was also everything you are and everything that we're going to be together."

The box in his hands hits the pavement.

"Damn, baby," he rasps.

"I hope that wasn't breakable," I say lightly.

"I'll replace it."

"I can be bribed with chocolate chip cook—*ack!*"

One second, I'm on my feet.

The next, I'm in the air, being tossed over his shoulder as he hightails it to the stairs and starts carrying me up them.

"Fox!" I squeak. "What are you doing?"

A swat to my ass. "You." A beat. "And then I'm making you cookies."

Laughter in the air.

Love in my heart.

And the last thing I see before the door to my apartment swings shut is my uncle scooping up the box from the pavement and shoving it into the back of my car.

———

Thank you for reading! I hope you enjoyed this glimpse into Fox and Dessie's story! If you want to fall in love with more big, bearded hockey players, pick up book one in the Grizzlies Hockey series, MARRIED TO NUMBER TWENTY-TWO. **I signed the contract. I just didn't expect her to show up ten years later, ready to cash it in.**

CLICK HERE TO READ MARRIED TO NUMBER TWENTY-TWO NOW>

Read on for a sneak peek below!

AIDEN

I wake up to a heavy knock on my condo's front door and glare blearily at my phone in the charger.

"Two in the fucking morning," I mutter, grabbing a pillow and clamping it over my ears. "It's two o'clock in the morning on my fucking birthday, and I have to deal with this shit."

This shit being my neighbors.

It's not the first time they've pounded drunk on my door, desperate for their roommate to let them in to what they think is their apartment.

This was sort of funny the first time.

I remember those days, drinking too much, being dumb.

But after the second and the third—where I gained status into the inner circle and a code to the keypad to their apartment door —it was no longer cute.

Now, six months later and countless times of bailing them out, I'm *so* not in the mood.

Especially when it's my fucking birthday.

The knocking cuts off and I think—*pray*—that they've gotten the hint.

But it's approximately two seconds later when it starts up again.

I glance at my phone again, see that really five minutes have passed, making it two-seventeen and officially my birthday.

Some present.

I could try to ignore it—but that just means extending the torture. Sighing, I toss back the blankets and stomp to my apartment door, whipping it open to reveal a slender brunette on my doorstep.

"Ho, mama," she says, gaze taking a slow perusal down my body.

"Who the fuck are you?"

"It's me. Luna."

I stare at her, uncomprehendingly.

"From Rockfield?" she adds.

Recognition begins to dawn. "Luna Maybelle?"

"Yup! That's me." She nods, grinning, and I see it then, the glimpse of my best friend from the childhood rink I grew up playing at come out in her smile. Mischief and life. Joy and hard work.

Summers spent spending every spare moment together—her figure skating, me playing hockey.

But she's not little Luna anymore.

Christ, she's anything but—tall, beautiful, curves for days—and she's staring at me.

Because I'm staring at her.

Fucking hell.

I spur myself into motion.

"Luna! Oh my God!" I pull her into a hug. "What the hell are you doing here?"

"It's your birthday!" She holds up a piece of paper that looks faintly familiar. "And, well, it's mine too, remember?"

That's right.

We have the same birthday.

"We're both twenty-five, single, and—"

My eyes narrow in on the paper. It's crumpled and stained, as though it's years old.

A purple and pink swirl decorates the edges and suddenly I remember her painstakingly drawing it as we sat side-by-side at one of the high top tables of the ice rink, waiting for the Zamboni to finish cutting the ice.

Her brow had been furrowed. Her movements carefully controlled.

And I had been obsessing over how pink her lips were and

what her butt looked like in her skating dress, so much so that I barely remember what we'd been drawing.

No, I think hard, grabbing on to those memories, not what we'd been *drawing*.

The contract we'd put together.

The contract my hormonal twelve-year-old self had signed.

With a sparkly pink colored pencil.

A giant boulder settles in my stomach, but before I can snap myself out of the horror of those memories, she shoves the paper in my hands then throws her arms around my neck.

"We're getting married!"

CLICK HERE TO READ MARRIED TO NUMBER TWENTY-TWO NOW>

———

Have you met Lake Jordan, star forward for the Sierra, wedding officiant extraordinaire, and the man everyone hates to play against, and the woman who steals her way into his grumpy, broody heart? Lake and Nova's book, OVER THE LINE, is available now!

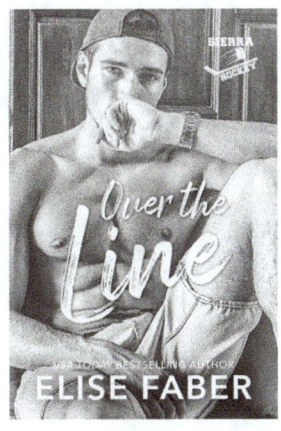

CLICK HERE TO GET OVER THE LINE NOW>

———

And don't miss my brand new hockey romance, BROKEN LACES. **I'm in love with the owner's daughter. But I can't have her...because if I do I'll lose everything.**
CLICK HERE TO READ BROKEN LACES NOW>

Hate missing Elise's new releases? Love contests, exclusive excerpts and giveaways?
Then signup for Elise's newsletter here!

www.elisefaber.com/newsletter

———

And join Elise's fan group, the Fabinators (https://www.facebook.com/groups/fabinators) for insider information, sneak peaks at new releases, and fun freebies! Hope to see you there!

———

If you enjoy my series, considering supporting me on PATREON! Get access to early releases, bonus content, character art, audiobooks, special edition covers, swag, and much more!

CLICK HERE TO SUPPORT ME>

———

I so appreciate your help in spreading the word about my books, including sharing with friends! Please leave a review on your favorite book site!

Rush Hockey

Also by Elise Faber

Breathless

Ballsy

Bewitched

Blowout

Breathe

Blazed

Sierra Hockey Series

Over the Line

Caught from Behind

The Big Skate

On the Fly

Rush Hockey Trilogy #1

Big Puck Energy

Filthy Puckboy

So Pucking Over It

Rush Hockey Trilogy #2

Love, Pucks, and Other Stories

All's Fair in Pucks and War

No Pucks Lost Between Us

Rush Hockey Novellas

Puck and Make Up

Eagles Hockey Series (all stand alone)

Broken Laces

Lace 'em Up

Knotted Laces

Loaded Laces

Lucky Laces

Billionaire's Club (all stand alone)

Bad Night Stand

Bad Breakup

Bad Husband

Bad Hookup

Bad Divorce

Bad Fiancé

Bad Boyfriend

Bad Blind Date

Bad Wedding

Bad Engagement

Bad Bridesmaid

Bad Swipe

Bad Girlfriend

Bad Best Friend

Bad Rebound

Bad Romance

Bad Business

Bad Billionaire's Quickies

Love, Action, Camera (all stand alone)

Dotted Line

Action Shot

Close-Up

End Scene

Meet Cute

Love After Midnight (all stand alone)

Rum And Notes

Virgin Daiquiri

On The Rocks

Sex On The Seats

Life Sucks Series

Train Wreck

Hot Mess

Dumpster Fire

Clusterf*@k

FUBAR

Perfect Storm

Free Fall

Lost Cause

Roosevelt Ranch Series (all stand alone, series complete)

Disaster at Roosevelt Ranch

Heartbreak at Roosevelt Ranch

Collision at Roosevelt Ranch

Regret at Roosevelt Ranch

Desire at Roosevelt Ranch

Phoenix Series (read in order)

Phoenix Rising

Dark Phoenix

Phoenix Freed

Phoenix: LexTal Chronicles (rereleasing soon, stand alone, Phoenix world)

From Ashes

In Flames

To Smoke

KTS Series (all stand alone, series complete)

Riding The Edge

Crossing The Line

Leveling The Field

Scorching The Earth

Cocky Heroes World

Tattooed Troublemaker

About the Author

USA Today bestselling author, Elise Faber, loves chocolate, Star Wars, Harry Potter, and hockey (the order depending on the day and how well her team -- the Sharks! -- are playing). She and her husband also play as much hockey as they can squeeze into their schedules, so much so that their typical date night is spent on the ice. Elise is the mom to two exuberant boys and lives in Northern California. Connect with her in her Facebook group, the Fabinators or find more information about her books at www.elise-faber.com.

f facebook.com/elisefaberauthor

a amazon.com/author/elisefaber

BB bookbub.com/profile/elise-faber

O instagram.com/elisefaber

J tiktok.com/@elisefaberauthor

g goodreads.com/elisefaber

www.ingramcontent.com/pod-product-compliance
Lightning Source LLC
Chambersburg PA
CBHW060333260626
47160CB00007B/2785